The Peter Pan Princess

A Novel by

Chely Schwartz

Stely Publishing

A division of Stely L.L.C.
©Copyright 2016

ISBN-13: 978-0-9914534-7-4
ISBN-10: 0-9914534-7-6

Author's photography by: Cari Baunn
Cover Design by: Design Infusions – David Ingram
Library of Congress Cataloguing-in-Publications
Data has been applied for.

Printed in the United States of America

Introduction

Operation Peter Pan
(Pedro Pan)

Between December 26, 1960 and October 23, 1962, 14,048 Cuban Minors were put on planes by their parents or family members, and sent to Miami, Florida. This mass exodus of unaccompanied Cuban minors was known as Operation Peter Pan, or as it was called in Spanish, Pedro Pan.

This operation was started by then director of the Catholic Welfare Bureau Father Bryan O. Walsh, and was inspired by a fifteen year old Cuban boy, who had immigrated to Miami from Cuba and was living with his relatives who were unable to provide for him. They asked the Catholic Welfare Bureau for assistance, and this triggered the idea to help many other young children to be able to immigrate to the United States in hopes of escaping the new government Fidel Castro was establishing in Cuba.

Many Cubans had heard, that this new government was going to send minors to the Soviet Union in order to serve in work camps, and this caused great panic in the Cuban families who were not able to emigrate. They felt the Castro regime was going to be short lived, so they sent their children to America to live with relatives already here, until they could be re united again, or to be cared for in shelters managed by the Catholic Welfare Bureau and in Foster care.

I encourage everyone to read about this very important moment in Cuba History, which occurred so very quietly, but needs a voice to be heard of loudly!

This book is a work of Fiction, but set in a real moment in time.   My hope is that it will bring attention to the actual facts and events during this period in time, and will bring a real face and story to everyone involved.

Dedication

This book is dedicated with Love and Admiration, to the 14,048 members of the Pedro Pan (Peter Pan) flights from Havana, Cuba, to America. And to the brave parents and family members who lovingly sacrificed to put them on those planes.

To my parents, my little brother Joe, and to the rest of my family, who left behind everything over fifty years ago, to start again with nothing. And whom with sacrifice, determination, great pride and hard work, have become the successful citizens of this country they are today.

To my Loves: My husband Steven, my children and grandchildren, and my son and daughter in law, for making my life so full and beautiful.

May our next generation **never forget** the reason this all happened. We came in search of Freedom, Democracy and Liberty.

God Bless America

The Peter Pan Princess

A Novel by: Chely Schwartz

Happiness, is something they say to hang on to. Love, is another thing they say, you should cling to if you are lucky enough to find it. Sara and Robert Bennis had both. They knew how lucky they were to have found one another, and they were very protective of their happiness.

Sara Morales was the daughter of a wealthy tobacco plantation owner in beautiful Pinar Del Rio, Cuba. It was the largest and most successful plantation in the region. Located in the countryside, it was thirty minutes outside the big city of Pinar Del Rio. The family had owned and worked the plantation for three generations. Most of the help had been there just as long. The Morales family treated them well and were very generous to everyone that worked for them and their families. It was unusual in those days, to have a 'Patron' with a heart such as Don Marcelino Morales and Doňa Maria Morales. They believed that if they took care of their employees, the employees would take care of them as well.

Doňa Maria made sure all of the children on the plantation got an education. The children went to school in a large 'Bohio' that had been built to accommodate all of them. A *Bohio* is a large house made of the branches and the leaves from the Royal Palms that are common in the beautiful lush Cuban countryside. The type of construction gave shade and comfort form the hot days in Cuba. Everyone received the best medical attention if they took ill. And there was always plenty to eat. The accommodations for the Campesinos, were humble but in excellent condition. It was rare that anyone left the employment at the Plantation "La Sonrisa". (The Smile) The Morales family was truly loved by all.

Robert Bennis was the son of a Jewish Diamond Cutter who owned a jewelry store in Havana. His parents had followed many other family members to Havana shortly after WW2. They were part of the Jewish Refugees from Antwerp. The Bennis family was part of the Jewish community that introduced the diamond polishing business to Havana, and employed hundreds of workers. They lived and worked near other family members, whom also owned many business in the Jewish sector of Havana. Some owned grocery stores, and others had general stores where they sold anything from religious items to cooked food.

Robert Bennis met Sara Morales while they were both at the University of Havana. She was there studying to become school teacher. He frequently sat under a large oak tree in the center of campus during his lunch break to eat and study. He'd watch her as she passed by on her way to class with her friends. Too shy to say anything, and knowing his family would never approve of his becoming involved with a Catholic, he'd only look at her and ponder about life being different.

On a rainy afternoon, Robert went to the Library to study. As he sat in a corner with his nose in a book, he heard a voice say, "Are you ever going to speak to me?"

Robert looked up and saw Sara taking the chair directly across from him, making herself at home without asking.

"I see you watching me every day. Aren't you ever going to say anything?" She said as she put her purse and her books on the table and took a seat. "I'm Sara Morales. What is your name?" she asked as she extended her hand to shake his.

Robert couldn't help but stare at Sara. She had long soft brown hair and the most amazing blue eyes he had ever seen. They shone with an incredible light as she smiled. Robert was so nervous he couldn't speak. He tried, but had difficulty forming words. Finally, he managed to raise his hand to shake hers and said, "I'm Robert Bennis. Pleased to meet you."

As his hand touched hers, Robert felt a chemistry like he'd never experienced. Still staring into her eyes, he continued to shake her hand until she said, "May I have my hand back please? Thank you".

"Your English is perfect. Aren't you Cuban?"

"Well of course. But I've been speaking English and French since I was a child. I attended Columbus School and was taught by American nuns. How is your Spanish?" She asked Robert as he stared at her with amazement.

"Muy Bien" he said. "I've been speaking Spanish since I was a boy. My family has businesses here, and they deal with many Spanish speaking Jews. I'm Jewish you know?"

"Really?" said Sara smiling and in a condescending way. "I would never had guessed. I just thought you were wearing the Yamaka as a fashion statement or to cover a bald spot on your head.

That managed to get a smile out of Robert. "I'm studying Accounting. What is your major of study?"

"Education. I love children. I plan to have a whole litter someday. Do your like children?"

"Yes I do. I love them too. I'm the middle one in my family. I have an older brother and a younger sister. Do you have any brothers or sisters?"

"No. My mother said I was such a difficult child she didn't want to take any chances of going through that again. She said she didn't get an hour of sleep for the first two years of my life. I don't understand that. I love to sleep now. I live with my Tia (aunt) Rosa and my Tio (uncle) Javier while I study. I'm actually form Pinar Del Rio. My Tia Rosa is my mother's sister. My Tio is a doctor here in the Havana. They didn't have any children. So they love it when I come to stay with them. I guess I'll be going back home after I graduate in June. But I'm not sure. When do you graduate?"

"June also. I'm staying here in Havana. I'll have plenty of work when I'm finished. I'm going to help my uncle in his accounting firm. He's getting along in years and needs me to give him a hand. Eventually, he'll retire and I will remain."

The conversation between Robert and Sara was easy, and it seemed to flow without any difficulty. It seemed they had a lot in common and were interested in one another's life and cultures. They talked and laughed to the point that the librarian had to *shush* them a few times. They continued to sit in the corner whispering to one another until it was time to close at 9:00 PM.

"Oh my goodness, my Tia is going to kill me! I must catch the bus. She'll be wondering what happened to me. I have to hurry home so I don't miss supper. Will you walk with me to the bus stop?" She asked with a smile he was starting to get used to.

"Of course. I have a bicycle outside. I'll go with you and wait until you're picked up."

"Thanks, let's hurry. I think the busses come every fifteen minutes or maybe less."

Sara watched as Robert untied the rope that secured his bicycle to a sign, and they walked hurriedly to the bus stop. Just as they got there, the bus pulled up and they said their good nights. Sara hung her head out the window and waved as the bus pulled away. Robert stood there wondering what had just happened. He'd never really had a conversation wth a female before, unless it was a relative. This was not part of their culture. But he was intrigued, and had a feeling of happiness inside that he had never experienced. As he jumped on his bike and began to peddle home, he wondered if he would ever have the opportunity to talk with Sara again. He knew that in his culture, often times marriages were arranged between parents. He wondered if the wife his parents would select for him would be as interesting as he found Sara to be. He also wondered if he and his bride would even have as much in common, as he had found with Sara. And he worried about the bride they might select. Would she even be as attractive as he thought Sara was beautiful? *It would be a shame,* he thought, *if I got stuck married to an ugly woman! OY!*

Chapter 2

"Tia, I'm sorry I'm so late. I was at the library and lost track of time. I'll get changed for supper and be right out."

Tio Javier was already seated at the head of table, and had begun placing his napkin into his collared shirt as to not get food on it. He had changed out of his usual white suit. No matter how much he tried, he always managed to get soup on himself. This was his way of trying not *wear* his dinner in case someone came by to visit, as was the custom in old Havana. He had arrived from the hospital at eight and had washed up for supper. He never wore his work shirt to the dinner table. Tia Rosa wouldn't allow it. She always felt he should not bring germs into the house, so she'd make him clean up before she'd let him sit down to eat. Tio Javier was a jolly grey haired man in his late fifties, who always had a smile and good things to say about everyone. He enjoyed his food very much as was apparent by his rounded middle. Tia Rosa was a pleasantly plump and very happy lady. When she smiled, her light brown eyes squinted so, that they seemed to disappear. Also in her mid-fifties. She had begun to grey early and had a silver streak that started on the left side of her scalp and spread as it went to the back of her head. Her hair was always pinned up, and never out of place. She always wore button down cotton dresses, usually in pastels or white, that were perfectly starched and ironed. Sadly, they had not been able to have children of their own. Tio Javier had evidently had a very bad case of the measles as a child and nearly died. They had attributed his infertility to that occurrence. But never the less, loved all of their nieces and nephews. Sara was their favorite. So when she decided to go to the University of Havana, they were very excited to have her stay with them in their home. Spoiling her as if she was their own.

Sara wasted no time washing up and sitting at the table. Tia Rosa and the lady who lived with them as their maid began to bring the food from the table. They placed a large soup terrine in front of Tio Javier, and the rest of the food throughout the table. There was always a fresh loaf of Cuba bread for Tio Javier to cut.

Tia Rosa sat at the table to the left of Tio Javier, and Sara directly across from her. Tio began to break up the bread while Tia Rosa ladled the soup into the bowls. Tio Javier asked Sara why she'd been so late?

"Well," she said as she began to eat her chicken soup, "I went into the Library because it started to rain and it was too early to go to the bus stop. I thought I'd get some reading done. Instead, I saw a boy there that I have observed watching me every day and never speaks to me. So I decided to approach him and ask him why he never had anything to say. I didn't understand why he never talks with anyone at the school. He always keeps to himself. At least, my friends and I never see him talking with anyone. He seemed very mysterious. It turns out, he is Jewish and doesn't seem to know any of the other Jewish students there. Not that there are many, but a few. He always eats his lunch under a tree in the School Park, reading and eating apples."

"Holy Jesus" said Tia Rosa as she made the sign of the cross, "A Jew. Sara does he know you are Catholic? Jews and Catholics don't really mix my dear. Did anyone see you talking to him? They always stick to their kind and you should stick to yours. That's just the way it's always been."

"But Tia," argued Sara. "He was really quite interesting. And it seems Jews and Catholics do have a lot in common. I enjoyed talking to him and hearing about his family and he seemed to like hearing about mine. He's very family oriented. He comes from a very close family. I told him all about you and Tio, and about Mama and Papa and the tobacco farm. That's why we lost track of time. I really liked talking to him. And he has the most beautiful brown eyes!"

"Sara no! I don't want to hear that kind of talk. You should stay away from him. Your parents would be very upset if they hear this kind of thing is going on while you are under our roof."

"Now Rosa," said Tio Javier lifting his spoon in the air and pointing it at her. "I was a Methodist when we first met, and hell didn't freeze over. They are just two young people having a conversation. It's not as if they were getting married. They are just talking. You are taking this much too far. Leave Sara alone. She's a smart girl and she knows what she's doing. Besides, I work with some very fine Jewish Doctors at the hospital and consider Dr. Rosenthal one of my closest friends. You have never had anything to say about *that*. Now let's finish our supper and I'll tell you about the twins I delivered this afternoon."

Sara smiled and thanked her Tio. Tia Rosa kept a Poker face and didn't have much more to say the rest of the evening. Later on, there was a knock at the door, and a couple who were good friends of them stopped by to visit. The men went out to the covered terrace to sit on the rocking chairs and smoke cigars and talk politics. The ladies went into the living room and talked about a

luncheon they were having for a mutual friend. Sara sat
by the opened window in her bedroom and began to read a
book. But she couldn't get Robert out of her mind. A
strong breeze began to blow through the light curtains,
and she could hear thunder in the distance. A storm was
fast approaching. She loved to sleep and listen to the rain.
So she crawled into bed and closed her eyes as she
listened to the rain get stronger outside her window. The
sound and the breeze finally put her to sleep. She slept
soundly all night.

When the morning sun woke her up, she hurried into
the bath. She was meeting friends. It was Saturday. They
had planned to go to the movies and they were meeting at
the bus stop at eleven that morning. "Casa Blanca" was
playing, and they were going to see the movie without the
sub titles. Sara and her two best friends, Ines and Sandra
liked doing this. It was good practice for them with their
English. They had all studied English in school since they
were little girls. And of course, the fact that Humphrey
Bogart was in the movie didn't hurt!

Sara and her friends met right on time. While traveling
to the theater, she told the girls of her encounter with
Robert. They all three giggled as young women do when
they talk about boys. Except at this age, they were now
really meeting young men and not boys. Soon they'd be

graduating and would be expected to marry. Ines already had a beau, and her parents were hoping she would start making plans to wed soon. Although they weren't officially engaged because she was still in school, it was understood this would happen right after graduation next June. Sandra had her eye on a young musician that her parents didn't approve of. But she was in no hurry to marry. She used to say she would rather be an Old Maid, than be made to cook or clean or do laundry. She wanted to travel before settling down. Sara was the only one that had always had her nose in her books. No boy had ever interested her before. So her friends were quite intrigued with her tales of Robert. She told her friends about the incident with her Tia Rosa the evening before. They both told her not to worry about it. They thought he was very good looking. And so what if he was Jewish. After all, it was 1942!

Chapter 3

As the months passed, Robert and Sara had become inseparable. But only during their time in school. Neither one of them had mustered up the nerve to tell their families, that they had fallen in love. Sara remembered the fit her Aunt had when she merely discussed talking to Robert. And Robert was afraid his parents would dis-own him, or that he would be shunned. The Christmas and Hanukkah seasons were fast approaching. The thought of being away from one another for the three week semester break was killing them.   And so they both decided it was time to have the families meet them. Robert would talk to his, and Sara would talk to her Aunt. She wasn't quite ready to tell her parents yet.

Sara stepped into her Tio's office one evening after supper and sat down on the chair across from his desk. Tio Javier looked up and slid his glasses to the tip of his nose. She looked at him nervously. Her hands were sweaty and she sat there wringing them. Tio Javier, being the smart man that he was, sat back in his big chair and said.

"It's about the boy isn't it? The Jewish boy?"

Sara looked shocked. "How did you know? How could you possible know?"

"Well Sara, I was once a young man too. Since that evening when you brought him up, I've had a feeling this young man was special to you. You've never discussed any young men in our home before. After all, you are at the age when these things come up. Are you in love?"

"Oh yes! We can hardly bare to be away from one another. I'd like to bring him home to you and Tia so the two of you can meet him. I don't want to go the Plantation for Christmas. I want to stay here to be close to him. You must meet him. He's a lovely person. He's smart and caring and funny and he has beautiful brown eyes. He comes from a wonderful close family like ours. Please, will you talk to Tia? Please convince her to at least meet him?"

"Well, you know that will take some convincing. But I have my ways. I'll talk to her. You ask your young man to come to Sunday supper. We'll have a look at him then."

Sara jumped out of her chair and went around the desk to hug her Tio. She thanked him and ran out the door to her room. She didn't want to be there when he spoke to her.

Robert went to visit his Zeydeh. That is what the

Jewish families traditionally call their Grandfather. He always went to him for advice. He was a wise and understanding man. And for a man of his eighties, he was very open minded. In his life time, he had experienced many changes in the world, and he knew that no matter how much you don't like it to, nothing ever remains the same.

Robert talked with Zeydeh. He told him of the beautiful Cuban girl who had stolen his heart and how he wanted to bring her home to the family. He said he hoped they would all love her as much as he did, because he wanted to make her his wife after graduation in June. Zeydeh told Robert that this would be a very difficult thing for his parents to accept. But that he would try to make them understand. These were different times, and modern young people sometimes take different paths than the ones parents wish for them. He would do what he could.

And so it was. Robert went to Sunday supper at Tia and Tio's house. He brought Tia a small pink box with Knish's to add to their Sunday meal. A Knish is Jewish pastries filled with potato. Tia Rosa apologized that they didn't have kosher food for him. But he explained that his family is more reformed and he did not always require his food to be kosher. The chicken she had fixed was

Delicious. The conversation between Tio and Robert was easy and laughter filled the room. Tia Rose watched the way Sara and Robert looked at each other. She knew this was true love. And she wondered how she was going to break the news to her sister and brother in law.

Sara also went to eat with Robert's family. She took them a box of Pastelitos that her Tia Rosa had made for his family. Pastelitos are Cuban pastries made out of phyllo dough filled with guava. Robert's mother came around right away. She was glad to see her son happy. His father was a bit more reserved about the whole situation. He thought the marriage may be cursed! But he too would eventually come around. Robert's brother and sister loved Sara right away and were very happy for him.

At Christmas time, Sara's parents came to Havana to spend the holiday with her and the rest of the family. Robert visited them and he asked for Sara's hand in marriage. He presented Sara with a one carat diamond in a beautiful but simple platinum setting. It was quite extravagant for the time. Everyone agreed to have the wedding in Havana by both a priest and a rabbi. Because of the nature of the unusual circumstances, the wedding was to be held at the Havana Country Club instead of a Church or a Temple, with only a small number of guests. Mostly immediate family. On the eve of the wedding, during a dinner celebration following the rehearsal, Robert's presented Sara with a small black velvet box containing her wedding gift. Inside, was a diamond and platinum brooch made by his father and uncle. The diamonds had been especially cut for her. She was to wear on her wedding day. Sara and her family were overwhelmed at their generosity. But she knew it wasn't just a gift from Robert, but a gesture of acceptance from his family.

On January 19, 1944, the small ceremony took place. The wedding couldn't take place on a Friday or Saturday in keeping with Jewish Sabbath. Sunday was out of the question, because Catholics attend mass that day. So, they met in the middle: Wednesday it was.

Sara was beaming as she walked down the aisle with her father. She wore a candle white dress made of the finest Spanish silk, hand sewn by her Tia Rosa. She also wore her mother's veil and her beautiful new brooch. Her parents had brought Gardenias from the plantation and the florist made her a lovely bouquet. She was a beautiful bride. The small room was filled with Roses, Lillis and Orchids.

After the ceremony, they all sat down to a huge meal. Both family's favorites were served. Robert and Sara were ecstatic. They were finally man and wife and could start their lives and family. They both wanted to have lots of children.

After the evening ended, they were driven to the Havana Hilton in a limousine. Robert carried Sara over the threshold. The evening would end the anticipation of their finally being together. Chaperones were still being used in Havana for single young women. Aside for hand holding and an occasional stolen kiss, they really didn't *know* each other.

Robert seemed more nervous than Sara. She was just excited and wanted to take the lead. She had seen way more movies than he had, so she had an idea of what she *thought* romance should look like. She began to try to unbutton her dress, but the buttons were too small and there were too many. So she asked Robert to help her. His hands shook. But when he finally managed to unbutton the dress, Sara turned and faced him. She slowly let the dress drop to the floor. She stood before him in a garter belt, her stockings and a camisole. Her breasts peeked from behind the satiny material. He could see that she was excited. Robert became even more nervous at the sight of his nearly naked wife. She was beautiful and shapely. He had never seen a nude woman before.

Sara began to help Robert undress. He managed to get his tuxedo jacket off, and his tie, but she was in a hurry to get to him. She slid his suspenders off of his shoulders and his pants dropped down around his ankles. She could see that he too was excited through his underwear. He pulled his shirt off over his head and began jumping around trying to get the pants off. He finally kicked his shoes off and managed to slip out of his trousers. There they were, looking at each other for the first time.

"I want to never forget this moment" Robert said to Sara. He took a step towards her and put his hand on her head, pulling the pins out of her hair. It slipped down her back and he ran his fingers through the strands. Sara ran her hands over Roberts's chest. She liked the long strands of dark brown hair that was growing around the top half of his chest. Then she slid her hand down. Robert tilted his head back, closed his eyes and took a deep breath.

"I've always wondered what a man looked like. I've seen little boys, but never knew what happened when they got older.

They both got a nervous laugh out of it. Robert then slipped the camisole off of Sara's shoulders. He could now see his wife. She was pure and beautiful. He pulled Sara close to him and put his face in her neck. He began to inhale her sweet scent. She smelled like her wedding bouquet. He then picked her up and placed her gently on the bed. He then joined her. Soon, with excitement, she cried out at the loss of the virginity. That which she had saved for her husband. Neither one of them felt any shame or inhibition. They were in love. They had waited for one another. They deserved to be happy and content.

After they finished making love and they lay there catching their breath, Robert asked Sara if she was all right.

They spent the next four days locked up in the room. Ordering room service and enjoying one another. It was splendor. It was amazing. It was a time of their lives they would never forget.

Chapter 4

Like any other couple, Robert and Sara had spent the first couple of years after their wedding making a home and starting their careers. Robert had purchased for them a spacious two story house in Havana not too far from where he worked. It had a beautiful patio in the center courtyard where there was always a lovely breeze. Every morning after breakfast on the patio with Sara, he would catch the bus near the house and rode it to work. Sara was within walking distance from the school where she taught Kindergarten. Their lives were filled with happiness.

Then, in the summer of 1947, they were blessed with a beautiful little girl. They named her Maribel. She was the spitting image of Sara. Her hair was light brown and wavy. She had her father's eyes and eye lashes. Light brown like a chestnuts. A radiant beauty.

Tio Javier and Tia Rosa had traveled to Pinar Del Rio to stay at the tobacco plantation with the family to await the birth of the baby. Sara had wanted her child to be born at her family home. She and Robert had arrived there a week before her due date. When the time came, Tio Javier delivered a seven pound eleven ounce bundle of joy to the family. Robert was filled with great emotion when Tio came out and placed her in his arms. Sara's mother Maria and Tia Rosa cried at the sight of her. Don Marcelino opened a bottle of champagne and poured glasses for all. He asked all of the help from the house to join them in celebration of the new member of the family. He then had bottles of wine taken to all of the homes of their workers so they too could celebrate along with them. He passed out a special cigar he'd had made to commemorate the great event. The birth of such a healthy beautiful little girl melted the hearts of everyone. Sara had an easy delivery. She labored only six hours.

Robert stepped into the room where Sara was, and thanked her. Both of them unwrapped the tiny baby and examined her to see what she looked like. She was perfect. Long tiny fingers like Sara's, tiny toes, and long eye lashes like Roberts.

"We should name her Maribel. We'll call her Mimi for short." Said Sara.

Robert was still crying at the sight of his new daughter. "My darling, you can call her anything you'd like. I'm just so happy that you are both all right."

Sara, Robert and Tia Rosa remained at the plantation for a month. Tio Javier returned to Havana after about a week to continue work in his practice. In those days, the mothers of newborns were allowed to rest and recover for long periods of time. She nursed the baby, and got up only to bathe and eat. Everyone doted on the baby. Robert was learning too about being a new father. He wanted to be able to help Sara as much as he could when they returned to their home. Sara was not going to return to teaching. She was going to be a stay at home mom. She would have some help around the house, but she wanted to be hands on with their little princess.

Mimi was a good baby. She slept well right off, and had no trouble eating. She ate every two hours at first, then three. This gave Sara a little more time to sleep between nursing. Especially during the night. She hardly cried, and loved to hear the sound of her parent's voice. Sara would get up in the afternoon after feeding Mimi and take her downstairs to play the piano softly for her baby. She would place her inside a cradle in the living room next to the piano. This was a grand room, with floor to ceiling windows that allowed the ocean breeze to flow across the room cooling it naturally. There were book shelves full of books, made out of mahogany that had been hand carved and brought over from Spain. There were several couches, and sitting areas with comfortable stuffed chairs. It was quite a palatial house. Mimi seemed to enjoy the sound of the soft lullabies Sara played for her. It was very soothing.

While the ladies were in the house, Don Morales would take Robert with him around the plantation to inspect the tobacco fields. The plantation was nestled in a large very lush green valley, surrounded by the three mountain ranges in Cuba. The mountains in Pinar Del Rio are very steep and made of limestone. They're a beautiful sight, visible between the plentiful Royal Palms that doted the property. On horseback, he liked to ride up and down the fields of the never ending plants. There was always a new crop of tobacco being cultivated and another being planted.

Because of the mild and constant climate in Cuba, and the humidity in the region, tobacco was grown there year round. Don Morales liked to inspect the leaves in the curing houses. The leaves were air dried in large open Bohios that allowed the air to filter through. They had to be cured for a year or more in order not have a bitter taste when they were rolled and smoked. He'd swing by the open Bohios where the tobacco makers, sat in long tables rolling the fine cigars that would be sold under the family brand. Other tobacco leaves were sold to exporters that would sell in trade all over the world. It was a busy business, and Don Morales was happy to visit with his workers every day. He made sure they stayed busy, but happy and well taken care of. He knew them all by name, and would always inquire about their other family members and children. Many of them had been at the plantation for several generations.

When Mimi was four weeks old, Sara and Robert returned with her to Havana. There, Robert's mother and sister stepped in to help Sara with the baby. They were enjoying their time with the little one as well. Robert was able to return to work content, knowing family was looking after his beloved Sara as well. He didn't want her doing too much and tiring herself. He treated her like a queen. Their love and respect for each other was undeniable. Robert adored Sara. He considered himself the luckiest man in the world to have her as his wife. Never expecting to marry someone like her. She was intelligent and witty. A real charmer. She was a good for him.

As Mimi grew, she became more and more beautiful every year. She was the almost identical twin of her mother. Her eyes were big, and her hair long and wavy. Sara would always comb Mimi's hair with a ribbon to match her dress. And she was always dressed beautifully. Mimi loved playing hide and seek with her Daddy in the courtyard when Robert got home from work. She would hide behind the large flower pots. He'd always pretend he couldn't see her. Laughter always filled their home. In the evenings, Robert would sit in his favorite chair and read. Sara would put Mimi on her lap and play the piano. Mimi liked to put her hands on top of Sara's while she played for Robert. She pretend that *she* was the one playing the lovely Cuban melodies that her Mami would play, and sometimes sing along to. Sara especially loved to play a new romantic song called - *Sabor a Mi.* To her, the words represented the deep Love that she and Robert had for one another.

Both the families loved the little girl. She was always spoiled when she visited Robert's family. And when they took her to the Plantation, whatever she wanted, she got. Don Morales even had a pony for her to ride around on.

On mother's day in 1951 when Mimi was four, Sara went to church in Havana with Tia Rosa and Tio Javier. Robert never attended Sunday services with them, but never denied her, her religion. After the service was over, they were standing in front of the church visiting with friends. Sara was holding Mimi's hand. Mimi was proudly showing everyone the picture she had colored for her Daddy and couldn't wait to get home and give to him. Sara let go of Mimi's hand for what was to be just a second to adjust her hat. Just then, Mimi's picture blew out of her hand. In a split second, she darted into the street to retrieve it. Sara yelled for her as she saw a street bus bearing straight at her child who was now bending over in the middle of the street. Without hesitation, Sara ran out after her and pushed Mimi out of harm's way. But for her it was too late. The bus had not slowed for a second, and ran Sara over in front of her family and church members.

It all happened so fast, it took time for everyone to react. Everyone was in disbelief. Mimi could be heard from the other side of the street screaming for her Mami. It was that sound that finally brought a reaction form everyone. Tia Rosa ran around the bus screaming, and retrieved Mimi. She covered her eyes and brought her back to where they had just been standing. Tio Javier and several other men were reaching under the bus to try to pry Sara out. But it was too late. Sara's body laid bloody and mangled and everyone cried out and screamed. Many broke out in prayer holding hands surrounding her remains. Tio Javier kneeled at her side sobbing uncontrollably. His white suit now red from all of the blood. The priest ran to try to console him, but he too was overcome at the sight of the beautiful Sara now gone to be with the Lord. Soon, the sound of an ambulance could be heard heading towards them. The people on the bus stepped out not knowing what had just happened and stood in disbelief on the sidewalk. It was a sad and tragic moment no one would ever forget.

Later that evening, Robert and his family sat with Tia and Tio at Robert and Sara's home, as they got up the courage to call Sara's parents at the plantation. Tio Javier could hardly speak the words as he told Don Morales that his beautiful daughter was gone. Robert was inconsolable. He sat holding Mimi close to him on his lap as he rocked back and forth. He didn't want to let go of her. It was all that he had of his Sara now. Roberts's mother tried to comfort him, but there was nothing anyone could say or do for him. His grief was unbearable.

After the funeral was over, and Robert's family held a Shiva in honor of Sara. Her remains were taken to the Plantation and buried in the family cemetery. There along with many of past generations of her family, she would be laid to rest in peace. Robert couldn't be torn away from the grave even to eat that day. No one saw him return to the house that night. They had all gone to bed and didn't see him come in.

In the late morning, Mimi sat playing on the floor of the living room at the Plantation. Roberts's family had left the afternoon before, right after the burial. Don Morales told Doña Maria that he needed some air, and got on his horse to go for a ride. It was close to noon when

Robert finally emerged downstairs looking very much disheveled. Mimi ran up to him calling Daddy, Daddy. He bent over to pick her up and gave her a kiss. As he stepped into the living room, Doňa Morales called for the cook to bring him some breakfast and coffee.

"No thank you Mama. I'm not hungry right now." He said as he put Mimi down and dropped down into a chair.

Doňa Maria pointed a finger at him and said, "You need to eat Robert. You have hardly touched food in a week. No one is happy, but we all have to go on. Look at your daughter. You have to take care of yourself for her. We all have to take care of ourselves so we can be there for her. Sara wouldn't want you to be this way. She loved you and would want you to go on. She was my only child. I miss her with every breath I take. I know we will never see her again, but look at that face." Maria pointed at Mimi. "There is Sara. In your daughter. We will always see her there."

"That is something we need to talk about. I don't know what to do or how I am to take care of her. I have my work. I can't take a small child with me every day to my office while I look at numbers and balance sheets. How am I to do this? Why am I being tested this way? I've always tried to be a good man. How can God do this to me, or to us?"

"Robert, why don't you leave her here with us until you figure things out? You can come on the weekends to be with her. That way you can decide who she can stay with in Havana. I'm sure Tia Rosa can help some, but she's getting older and can't chase around after such a bundle of energy every day. You will need some help. Perhaps a Nany can help or you're Mother?"

"My Mother I'm sure would love nothing more than to help take care of Mimi. But her back is very bad and can't stand for long periods of time. She can't bend over to pick her up and carry her. Believe me, this is breaking her heart as well. I think the best thing for Mimi right now is for her to remain on the plantation with you until things settle down. Besides, I think it would be too difficult for her right now to try to understand why Sara isn't home, or that she isn't ever going to come home if she's there. She's just too young. Eventually she'll have to figure it out on her own. But she's just too young to have had this happen to her. Thank you for offering to keep her temporarily. I still have to go through the house. Tia Rosa has offered to help me next week get Sara's things packed away. I need some time to grieve on my own as well."

The cook entered the room and placed a tray on a table next to Robert. Mimi walked over and offered to help him eat his toast. He placed her on his lap and began to take bites as she held them up for him. Maria watched silently, thinking how much Mimi looked like Sara at that age. It made her cry so she walked away. Stepping into the front porch to get some fresh air, she could see at a distance, her husband's horse tied to the fence that surrounded the family burial plot. She sat on a rocking chair and buried her face into her apron and cried. Life would never be the same for any of them. But they still had Mimi.

Chapter 5

Days, weeks, months and three years passed. Robert had been visiting Mimi at the Plantation often at the beginning. But as time progressed, his visits became rare. Mimi never went back to live in Havana with her father. He said it was because the older she got, the more and more she reminded him of Sara. Don Marcelino and Doňa Maria knew he had thrown himself into his work. The telephone conversations with Roberts's mother confirmed that he had been thrown into a deep depression after Sara's death. The only way he could really cope was to work. He kept long hours and never socialized with anyone. The house had become a shambled mess, and he had let the help go. Robert's mother would take him food to the office. If not for that, no one in the family would even see him. His uncle had retired now and he used that as an excuse that he was too busy.

Although Mimi missed her father, she was thriving at the Plantation. Her Abuelo and Abuela, (grandfather and grandmother) had hired a private tutor that came to the house every morning at nine and gave her lessons until noon. Every Monday and Wednesday, Doňa Maria would have their driver take her and Mimi into the city for ballet lessons in the afternoon. On Tuesday and Thursday, the piano teacher would come in at four and give Mimi piano lessons for one hour. Then, she was to practice for another hour then finished her studies from the morning and wash up for supper in the evening.

Mimi adored her grandparents. They loved her and gave her anything a child could want. She loved sitting at the supper table and listening to the two of them talk. Abuelo would tell Abuela all about the happenings at the plantation. The new crops, the sales. Who was picking up the cases of cigars and where they were being shipped to? A lot of them were going to America. This intrigued her. The tutor was teaching her to speak English. Mimi wanted to know why she had to learn this other language if she never got to go there. She would always ask questions about it. Her grandparents had been there many times and would tell her stories about all the different places they had gone to. She heard about a place called Miami, and New York and Niagara Falls. She especially liked to hear about Niagara Falls. One of the places Mimi wanted to go visit in America was called an "Automat". They told her that it was a kind of restaurant where you put coins into a little window and food or deserts would come out! That sounded amazing to her! Her big dream was to go to the Automat and get a ham sandwich out of one of those little windows. Her grandparents told her that they would someday take her on a vacation there. And that if she kept taking her piano lessons, she would be good enough to play at "Carnegie Hall" in New York. Abuela would show her albums of their trips, and show Mimi a photos of the stage at Carnegie Hall. Mimi loved looking at the albums. She told her Abuela that when she was good enough to go play there, she was going to move to New York.

One Sunday after church, Abuela had helped Mimi out of her best dress, braided her long hair into two braids and let her put on her play clothes. She went outside and sat on the porch. The workers didn't work on Sunday and everything was calm. Mimi sat quietly listening to the sounds of the birds in the trees and looking at the clouds. She liked finding figures in them. Suddenly out of nowhere, she heard someone laugh. It was the sound of a child giggling. She couldn't tell where it was coming from, so she decided to explore. As she walked down the path towards the tobacco fields, she heard a little whistle. She tried to follow that sound too. But every time she heard it, it was from another direction. Someone was playing with her. She began to run in and out of the rows of tobacco in the field she thought the sound was coming from. She could hear someone running too, trying to hide from her. Whoever it was, they were too fast and she couldn't catch them. This annoyed her so she said out loud.

"I don't want to play anymore. I'm tired. I'm going home." She turned on her heals and started back towards the porch, and as she did, she felt someone pull on one of her braids. She turned around and found a little boy about her age standing there smiling at her.

"Who are you?" she demanded. "You aren't supposed to be here. If my Abuelo finds out that you aren't with your family and with the other workers you're going to be in big trouble."

"My name is Antonio Enrique Reyes at your service. I know who you are. You are the little Patrona, Mimi."

"Patrona? No one has ever called me that. They just call me Mimi. My Abuela is the Patrona."

"I know. My Abuela asked me to bring some bread to the big house for your supper. She just baked it and wanted your family to enjoy some of it. I went to the back door and gave it to the cook lady Berta. Then I saw you when I was walking back home. Do you want to see my fort?"

Mimi looked at him with a smile. "I don't know what a fort is. What is it?"

"Come, I'll show you. But you can't tell anyone. It's a secret fort. Do you promise to keep it a secret?"

"Yes, I promise." Mimi made the sign of the cross to show she was serious about keeping Antonio's secret. She'd never been asked to keep a secret by anyone before. Really she wasn't even sure what a secret it was. But she thought it was something that she must never tell anyone.

Antonio walked ahead towards the back of the property. When they got to the fence, he lifted the wire that was loose near the ground and he slipped through holding it up so Mimi could crawl under it as well. He kept going until he got to the line of big trees about twenty yards from the fence.

"Come on." He said looking back at Mimi. It's not far now."

Mimi followed behind, but she kept looking back to where they had just come from. She'd never been this far from the house before. But it was exciting to her. She was on an adventure. It was fun!

They finally reached a small creek, and Antonio skipped across it. There were stones he stepped on to get to the other side. He reached back for Mimi's hand and said to her.

"Here, hold my hand. Just step where I've stepped." When they got to the other side, he pointed up to the top of a big tree and said, "There it is. Up there."

Mimi looked up in the direction he was pointing. She could see some cardboard and some planks about half way up the tree. "How are we getting up there?" She asked.

"I have a rope. We just climb up the rope." With that, Antonio grabbed a rope that was hanging from the back side of the tree and began to climb. There were big knots every several feet to make it easy to hang on to. He finally got to the top and hollered to Mimi to do what he'd done to climb up. Mimi did as she'd been asked to do. At first a bit slow, but she got the hang of it. When she got near the top, he reached down and grabbed her arm, pulling her inside. Once they were both in, she took a look around.

"Wow!" That's a nice view from here. You can see some of the valley and most of the plantation. How did you find this place?"

"My older brothers built it when they were my age. They used to come and play here. But we never told our parents about it. So it's a secret place. They used to bring me here when I was little. Now they are older and left home. One of my brothers is away studying in the city. My older brother got married and lives in Matanzas with his wife. They're going to have a baby soon. I'm going to be an uncle. Do you have any brothers or sisters?"

"No. It's just me. My Mom died when I was little and my father lives in Havana. He doesn't come to see me much anymore. But he calls sometimes."

Antonio stood and walked towards the back of the fort. "Do you like sugar cane? I have some. It grows wild near here."

"I've had it before, but my Abuela says the sugar isn't good for my teeth."

"Let me cut some up. We can suck on the cane and watch the birds. They have nests up here and sometimes you can see the babies when they are getting fed."

Antonio grabbed a long piece of sugar cane and grabbed a big knife he had underneath a small chair. This took Mimi by surprise, but so did everything else her new friend had done so far.

Antonio cut two twelve inch pieces off of the big stalk and began to carve off the outer covering. They each got a piece and sat near a window. They sat quietly sucking on the delicious sugary cane, and watched as a pair of parrots squawk and walked around their nest. Their colors were bright and their beaks were big. Mimi was completely enthralled in the view. This was all new to her. She'd never been away from the big house and into the forested area before. She was definitely going to keep the secret of the fort.

After a while, Antonio told her he'd better get her back before anyone missed her. He didn't want her to get into trouble. He didn't want to get into trouble either. When they got to the other side of the fence, Mimi said to Antonio.

"Will you come to see me again? Will you be my friend? I don't have anyone to play with here and I had a fun time with you today."

"I don't know." He responded. I'm not supposed to be on this side of the plantation unless I'm with an adult. We're supposed to stay on our part of the property unless we're working."

"I will ask my Abuela if it's ok. But I won't tell her about the fort. I'll just say that you are a nice boy and I like talking with you. I'm sure she will say it's all right."

"Well, if it's alright with her, then I will be your friend."

Antonio brought up his hand to shake hers. They shook hands and went their separate ways.

That evening when they sat down to supper, Berta placed the loaf of bread on the table that had been sent over by Antonio's family. Mimi took this as a perfect opportunity to introduce the idea of her friendship with him.

"Abuela, may I have a friend here on the plantation?

The girls in ballet class all live in the city and I only see them during class. I don't have anyone to play with."

Doña Morales look puzzled at Mimi and asked. "Who would you play with here? The only children are the children of the workers. They live on the other side of the plantation. I'm not sure anyone of them would be interested in coming here just to play with you. You don't even have anything in common with any of them."

"I met one today. The boy that brought the bread on the table. His Abuela baked it for us. He's very nice. We talked about all kinds of things. Like the birds in the trees and his family. I would like it if he would be allowed to be my friend. Please Abuela?"

Don Morales looked at his wife and shrugged his shoulders indicating that he didn't really care if the boy came around once in a while.

"I suppose it would be all right. I'll have to have your Abuelo go and speak to his family to tell them it's ok for him to visit. But not during the week. You have your studies and your classes. You must keep up with your piano lessons or you'll never get to Carnegie Hall!" They all laughed at that statement. Mimi was happy that she would now have a real friend. Someone to talk to.

When they finished their supper, they all went into the living room. Abuelo sat by the radio as he did many times in the evening. He liked to light up a cigar and listen to "The Voice of America." Or to "Radio Swan." Abuela would read. Mimi played jacks, or paper dolls until it was time to go to bed. This night when she said her prayers, she was also grateful that she was going to have a friend now. She couldn't wait until the next Sunday so she could see Antonio again.

Chapter 6

From that point forward, every Sunday afternoon, Antonio came to play with Mimi. They would play on the swing Abuelo had built for her in the front yard. They would ride on her pony, or just run abound like kids of seven and eight do. Sometimes they would skip rope. Abuela would hold one end, and the two of them would take turns turning the other end while they jumped. Other times, they would go into the house and take turns reading fairy tales to each other or play board games. Mimi liked to show Armando photographs of her grandparent's travels, or look at books with pictures of other countries. They wondered what kids from different parts of the world were like. Then Mimi would play the piano. Antonio loved to hear her play, and so did Abuelo and Abuela. She was really very talented. It seemed to come easy to her. When she played, her face seemed to change. It' as if she was being enthralled by the music. Almost as if she were in a trance. Her music was that of someone well beyond her age. She was truly amazing.

Other times, they would just play hide and seek in the tobacco fields, and when they could, they would sneak away to the fort or go play in the water from the creek. They had become best friends.

In 1959 just before Mimi's twelfth birthday, things in Cuba began to change. People seemed to be more serious, and less at ease about life. Castro had overthrown the then leader of Cuba, Fulgencio Batista. He marched in the streets of Havana declaring himself Prime Minister of Cuba. From that point forward, Cuba became a totalitarian state.

Although most of what was happening was more concentrated in Havana, the people of the city of Pinar Del Rio seemed to become more and more affected. There was always whispering. Not as many people were out in the streets. After a while, some of the workers of the tobacco plantation seemed to just disappear. Mimi was told they moved away, but no one really knew where they had gone to.

Food was now being rationed in town. Everyone had been issued a book they would take to certain locations on certain days of the week. People would have to stand in line to buy whatever the government would ration out that week. Most of the time, food would run out before they could get to the front, and they would have to wait until the next time it was their turn to buy food. Living on the plantation, the workers weren't affected much. Don

Morales always made sure they all had plenty to eat. A portion of the plantation was farmed. And there were cows, chickens and pigs. Food was never a problem for them. And Mimi never had a hungry day in her life. It seemed strange to Mimi who was growing up in her own little world. She didn't understand what was happening, but could definitely pick up that life wasn't like they used to be. But her Grandparents continued on as if nothing was going on. They didn't want her affected by what was happening in the world. After all, they had lived through government changes before in their life time. Sometimes, things like this were just temporary.

In October of that year, Robert called the Plantation asking to speak with Mimi. He told her that he was going to move to America. He said that he that he would see her soon. Then he spoke with Don Morales and explained that the 'Fidelistas' were starting to persecute the Jews. They were told that their businesses were now the "property of the state" and had begun to confiscate everything they owned. Many were being thrown in the streets with nothing. The ones that protested, were being beaten or shot in front of their families. They were made examples of to the others. Robert and his parents had decided to get out before things got worse. He told Don Morales that he would let them know where he was as soon as he had a permanent address, as they were taking a leap of faith and just leaving not knowing where they would end up. This terrified Don Morales. He confessed this to his wife later that evening after Mimi had gone to bed. They decided they would have to prepare for the worse, and try to do what was best for Mimi.

The next couple of years, things went from bad to worse. By 1962, Don Morales lived by the radio day and night. Listening to the intently for word of what was happening, as told by programs outside of Cuba. Hearing of horrible things that were happening to the people of Cuba. People being thrown in prison, or executed for being 'Anti-Castro'.

Mimi's fifteenth birthday was fast approaching. She'd been asking what was going to be done about her Quinceañera. That was a custom. A formal birthday party given a young lady when she turns fifteen. Like a rite of passage. She had asked her Grandparents if Antonio could be her escort for the party. But they hadn't had the heart to tell her there would be no party. Most of the family friends had already left Cuba. Many gone to Spain, Mexico or Venezuela. Some moving to America. There was no one really to invite.

One Sunday evening at supper, they sat Mimi down and tried to explain to her in a very basic way, that life in

Cuba was not the life that existed when she was a little girl. And that they may have to make some decisions very soon about perhaps leaving the island. Her Abuelo had heard on the radio about the "Peter Pan" flights. The Peter Pan program had been under way since 1960. Parents were sending their children to Miami, to family members or friends who already lived in America. They explained to her that the Catholic Church was helping to take care of the children until they could be reunited by their other family members that were to follow. A Priest by the name of Bryan Walsh of the Miami Diocese and the State Department of the United States had special waivers giving these children special visas, and that Tio Javier and Tia Rosa were working on getting one for her. They told Mimi that she would have to leave first, and that they would get word to her father so he could go after her until they were able to come to join her.

Mimi began to cry. No party? And now, her world was being turned upside down. She didn't want to leave her elderly Grandparents. She loved them so much. She couldn't bear the thought of leaving them behind. She was afraid she would never see them again. The thought of leaving her homeland without any one in her family terrified her. She went to her room without touching her food. She sat on the floor in her room crying. After a while, she heard a soft whistle from down below. She knew it was Antonio. Sometimes late Sunday nights, he would sneak over when everyone had gone to bed and she would climb out the bedroom window and down the trellis. They would go for a walk, or sit on the swings and talk. He had told her that there was going to be a meteor shower that night and that he would come get her at midnight so they could watch.

Don Morales and Doña Morales stayed in the living room nervously listening to the radio until late that night. She told her husband that she had reservations about letting Mimi go. They had kept her too isolated and that Mimi was very naïve. She knew nothing about the real world. Mimi was used to having everything done for her. Even dressing. She had the help picking out her clothes to get her dressed in the morning, and she herself would go help Mimi wash up and put on her nightgown and brush her beautiful long wavy hair. They peeked in Mimi's room before going to bed. Mimi pretended to be asleep. She laid there and waited to hear the soft whistle from her friend.

Shortly after midnight, she heard the sound of her friend coming to get her. She threw her bathrobe over her night shirt and climbed out the window and down the trellis as she always did. Antonio had a blanket, and they ran into the night behind one of the tobacco rolling Bohios. As they laid there waiting to see the star show, Mimi told Antonio of the conversation she had that evening with her grandparents. She told him she didn't want to leave him because she loved him. Antonio looked deeply into Mimi's eyes and told her that he had planned on making lots of money and marrying her someday. He told her that he loved her too, and that nothing could ever change that. Antonio and Mimi sat up, and shared their first kiss. It was soft and gentle. The kiss of innocence. They held hands and watched the meteors shoot by for hours before returning to their homes. Mimi laid there thinking about her first kiss, and how special it had been. Armando was her first friend, and now was her first love. She would always treasure that night, and wished time would go by faster so they could grow up and be married.

A week later, Doña Morales and Mimi were in the city for her ballet lessons. There was now just a hand full of girls left. Many of them had just disappeared. While they were in the city, a convoy of five green military jeeps ripped through the countryside and up to the main house. Don Morales stepped outside only to find himself looking at twelve military soldiers dressed in green uniforms with rifles, getting out of their vehicles.

"What is it you want? There is nothing for you here."

Said Don Morales in a very authoritarian manner.

"Quite the contrary. We are here to inspect the property that belongs to the government. This plantation is now owned by the Revolution. Who are you?" Asked the man who seemed to be in charge. The rest of the men stood pointing their rifles at Don Morales.

"I am Don Marcelino Morales I'm the owner of this property and you are trespassing."

By then, many of the field workers had stopped what they were doing and were watching terrified at the soldiers that had ridden in on the jeeps.

The man who addressed Don Morales walked up to him on the porch and pushed him down. Then he proceeded to walk into the house. Don Morales tried to get up, but three of the men ran up to the porch and pointed their riffles right at his chest. Several more of them walked into the house right behind the first one. They began to look through things and lighting some of the cigars that were in a humidors on top of the piano. One of them even sat on the piano and began to bang on it with the barrel of his gun. Berta the cook watched in horror from the kitchen door.

After about an hour, they came out of the house. They had the humidors full of cigars under their arms.

"Look here *Don Morales,*" Said the officer with a

condescending voice. "We will be back here day after tomorrow. You have only one choice. You will move out of this house and into one of the workmen's houses, and you will continue to produce the crops for the government. You are no longer "Patron". You are just a worker for the state. And you work for the Revolution now. If we find you taking anything, from this plantation, anything at all, you will be shot. Am I making myself clear?"

With that, he took a cigar out of his shirt pocket, bit off the tip and spit it at Don Morale's face. He turned and they all got in their jeeps. As they rode off the property, they began shooting their rifles in the air. The workers were terrified. Don Morales tried to stand up. Several of the workers came to help him to his feet.

"Back to work everyone. Everything is going to be all right. Don't worry about anything. We'll be fine. Go back to your work. I'll handle everything."

Several hours later when Doňa Maria and Mimi returned after ballet lessons, she found Don Morales in the house sitting in his favorite chair in the living room. He was drenched in sweat, and pale as a ghost. Berta had brought him some ice water and was standing there with a kitchen towel fanning him.

"Marcelino! What's happened? Are you all right?" She asked when she entered the house.

Don Morales waved at Berta and asked her to take Mimi into the kitchen for something to drink. She did as she was told, as she knew he was wanting to speak with his wife in private.

Doňa Morales sat in a chair across from her husband and listened to him describe the events of that afternoon. He spoke in a very low tone, as he didn't want anyone to hear their conversation. She sat there in horror, listening to her husband. She knew they had gone as far as they could with Mimi, that and it was time to get her out of the country. They were afraid of what could happen to her when the soldiers came back. A beautiful young lady that. God forbid! So, they called Havana and spoke with her sister Rosa and her husband Javier. They made plans to meet that very same night in San Cristobal. About half way between Pinar Del Rio and Havana.

Don Morales called for his driver and asked him to be at the plantation house at eight o'clock that night. Both of them walked upstairs to talk to Mimi and explain things to her. As they entered the room, Mimi was sitting on her bed shaking. She had anticipated something was terribly wrong from the minute she had returned from her ballet class.

"What is happening? Please, tell me. I'm going to be fifteen in two days. I'm not a little girl any more. I want to know what is going on?" She pleated with her grandparents.

As they began to try to explain things to her, she became more and more hysterical. They told her she would have to leave that night, and she would be staying with her Tia Rosa and Tio Javier until she could get on the Peter Pan flight to America. Shaking her head no, and pacing up and down her room, Mimi protested and cried. Her grandparents both crying and trying to re assure her that everything would be all right. But something inside of Mimi told her that things were not going to be all right, and that her life was about to change drastically.

Abuela took a small suit case out of Mimi's closet and began to place things inside. She knew there would be a limit to what she would be able to take, so she was careful to pack necessary clothing and nothing Mimi wouldn't need right away. She set out clothes for Mimi to change into for the trip to Havana. Mimi stood there crying like she had never cried in her life. At eight that evening, Abuelo walked Mimi out to the car, and Abuela told her good bye. They hugged one another and she tried to re assure her that everything would be ok. She kissed her forehead and closed the car door. Mimi looked at her from inside and waved bravely. As the car drove away into the night, Maria looked up into the sky and said a prayer. She asked God to help her, and then prayed to her daughter's angel to be with Mimi.

Hours later, they arrived at the rendezvous location. By then, Mimi had gone into shock. She had stopped crying, but had also stopped talking. Once she saw her uncle's car, she knew it would be the last time she would ever see her grandfather. It was a gut feeling she would never forget. Saying good bye to her grandfather was the hardest thing she'd ever had to do in her young life. They embraced one another with the same longing feeling, but knowing how very truly they loved one another.

Tia Rosa sat in the back seat with Mimi while Tio Javier drove back to Havana. Mimi didn't speak very much on the drive home. She wished it wasn't dark so she could see out the window. If she was to go live in America, she was unsure if and when she would see this countryside again.

By the time they arrived back in Havana, the sun was just creeping over the horizon. They were all tired. Rosa put Mimi to bed in the room her mother stayed at when she lived with them. Tia Rosa offered something to eat, but she shook her head no. It was all happening too fast. She never got to say good bye to Antonio. She was crushed. Leaving her grandparents, her home, and the boy who was her best friend and whom she loved all in such a short period of time was too much to bare She fell asleep almost immediately.

Chapter 7

Two days after Mimi left, Don Morales was in one of the tobacco rolling Bohios watching as cigars were being rolled for a special order. He walked up and down the tables visiting with all of the 'Torcedores'. That is the name given to the men and women who roll the cigars. The day was progressing like any other day, until around eleven that morning, when they all heard the sound of the military jeeps come rolling onto the property again. Everyone stopped what they were doing. Don Morales stepped outside to confront the men as they stepped out of the vehicles. The captain who had threatened him before, had pulled his jeep right up to the front of the house. He stepped out and turned to meet Don Morales as he charged towards him, yelling at him.

"Get off of my property." As he approached, the soldier pulled out a hand gun and shot Don Morales in the center of his chest. He was dead almost instantly.

Hearing the sound of the gunfire, Doňa Morales ran out of the house screaming. She ran towards her dead husband and held him as he took his last breath. The soldiers just stood there and pointed their guns towards all of the workers as they walked outside and witnessed the killing of their beloved Patron. Doña became so infuriated at the man who had shot her husband that she began to run towards him with her fists in the air, ready to take him on. But when she got closer, he took aim and shot her too. She died instantly. Berta the cook witnessed this and ran inside crying, through the house and out the back door, all the way to where she lived. The rest of the workers stood frozen. The soldier yelled at them to drag the bodies and throw them in with the pigs. At first, no one moved, but when they began to shoot their guns in the air, several of them finally stepped forward and reluctantly did at they were told.

The soldier walked up to his jeep and stood on the hood. He began to give a speech addressing all of the workers on the plantation. They were told that *he* would be moving into the house to oversee the plantation, and that they were now working for the revolution. He threatened them not to leave, or to take anything from the farm for their own use. They were told that from now on, their food was going to be rationed like everyone else's, and anyone caught stealing anything from the garden or even stealing a single egg, would meet the same fate as their old patroness. He then put his fist up in the air and yelled, "Viva Fidel!" When no one responded, he started to shoot at their feet telling them to respond. He tried it again, "Viva Fidel!" This time, the men and women that were present all responded in the same manner. This was the common totalitarian indoctrination the Fidelistas used on everyone. And if you were caught doing anything they didn't like, they would shoot you in the head without even thinking twice. This was life from then on, for everyone who lived there. At least for anyone not brave enough to escape.

Back in Havana, unaware of what had just occurred, Mimi woke up and came into the dining room. Tia Rosa greeted her.

"Good morning. Are you hungry?"

"No, I don't want anything to eat."

"But my dear, you should eat something. You can't survive on air. You haven't eaten since you got here. Here, sit at the table. I know this has all been very hard on you, but you will see. Things will be all right. When you get to Miami, you'll have an envelope to give to the people who are there to greet you. It will have your father's contact information. They'll let him know you have arrived, and he'll come and take you to his house. He's a very nice man. And he loves you very much."

"If he loves me so much, why did he leave me? Why couldn't he let me live with him in his house after my

Mother died?"

Tia Rosa looked at Mimi. Her eyes filled with tears.

"Mimi, you parents were very much in love. Your mother's death devastated your father. He was in no mental condition to take care of himself, much less a little girl. Don't fault him for that. He did what he thought was best for you. It wasn't easy not having you with him. But he wanted you to be with family instead of just a Nany while he was at work. He worked very long hours. Wasn't your life with your grandparents wonderful?"

"Yes, but I wished we could have been closer. I missed him very much. Now, I'm not sure I even remember what he looks like. How will I know what he looks like when I see him in America?"

Tia Rosa rose from the table and walked over to a cabinet. She pulled out a photo album and walked over where Mimi was seated and placed it in front of her.

"Here, look through these photos. They're photos of your parents, and of you with them. Perhaps this will help you to remember. I'm going to go into the kitchen and get you some milk and toast."

Mimi sat there turning the pages. There were photos of her parents at their wedding. And photos of the three of them. Some were of her first birthdays, and of them playing outside in the patio of their home. There was one she especially liked. It was of her on her mother's lap with her hands on hers, as she played the piano.

"I remember doing this with her. She used to let me put my hands on hers when she played. Now when my fingers touch the keys, I feel like I'm channeling her somehow. May I have this one Tia Rosa?"

"Of course you can. Take it with you."

As they sat looking at the rest of the photos and eating toast, Tio Javier came through the doors into the dining room in a furry.

"I have it! I have it!" He said as he waved a yellow piece of paper up in the air.

"What do you have?" Asked Mimi with a puzzled look on her face.

"I have your special Visa. You leave tomorrow morning. We have to be at the airport by seven in the morning."

Tia Rosa and Mimi looked at one another. They were in shock. They both thought there would be more time to spend together, but *there* it was in his hands. Mimi was leaving for America on her fifteenth birthday.

Tio Javier walked over to Mimi and handed her the yellow piece of paper. What Mimi didn't know was just how much that little yellow piece of paper was about to change her life forever. She read it over and over. Sure enough, it was tomorrow's date. July 14, 1962.

"Tomorrow is my birthday. I won't have a birthday this year. It'll all be spent travelling to some place I've only heard of."

Tia Rosa stood and said, "Well, we can't have you going off without a celebration isn't that right Tio? I'm going to go bake you the best birthday cake you'll ever have!"

With that, she went running into the kitchen. Tio asked Mimi if there was anything she wanted to do on her last day in Havana.

"I'd like to go see my old house. Will you take me to go see it? I remember it not being too far from here."

"Come with me. We'll take a walk over there right now."

Mimi and Tio Javier walked the four blocks to a corner and turned left. On the next corner, stood a house with a porch and big windows. It looked to be abandoned and boarded up. All of the trees and shrubs were over grown. The rose bushes were drooping and dead. Mimi pushed the Iron Gate open, and they stepped inside. They walked up the steps to the porch and looked in through the cracks on the boards that had been nailed on to protect the windows. She could see the inside of the house was empty and dirty. She saw the place where her mother's piano had once been. It brought tears to her eyes.

"Thank you Tio, but I've seen enough. Seeing my house like this makes me very sad. I don't want to stay here any longer. Let's go back to your house."

The two of them walked quietly back. Mimi felt her heart breaking. She felt as if everything she knew in her life up to this point was being taken away; and it was. She had been taken away from her home, and the two people she loved most in the whole world. Her childhood home was in ruins. And now, she would have to leave her beloved aunt and uncle. But what hurt most of all, was that she would now have to leave her homeland.

Back at the house, Tia Rosa had made a simple cake with what little ingredients she could find. They too had been hit with the food rationing. But she did what she could. That evening, after they finished eating, they sang to her. But Mimi could hear the sadness in their voices.

Chapter 8

It was still dark when Tia Rosa came in to wake Mimi up for her ride to the airport. But she was already awake. She had laid awake all night, nervous and scared about this day.

"Happy Birthday." Said Tia Rosa "You have to get up now. Tio will to drive you to the airport soon. Come, I'll help you get dressed and comb your hair."

"Aren't you going to go with me?"

"No. I'm not allowed. You can only have one person go with you. It'll be all right. I'll be here praying for you to have a safe trip. You send us a letter when you can and tell us how you are doing, and how your father is."

Not much was said after that. Tia Rosa took out of the closet a pretty pink cotton dress she had taken out of Mimi's suitcase the night before and had ironed it. Then she helped Mimi get her long wavy hair brushed. When they got down stairs, there was a glass with some juice for her and a piece of toast. Mimi could barely get the toast down. Her stomach was in knots.

"It's time to go my dear. You have to be there by seven." Said Tio Javier.

Mimi could hear the car outside. The engine was on. Tia Rosa's eyes began to tear up. Mimi was too chocked up to speak. Tia walked over to Mimi and gave her an envelope.

"Here is the information you will need to give to the people in Miami that will meet you at the airport. Most of them are from the Catholic Church, so you will be in good hands. Your father's name and address are in there. He'll take good care of you. He loves you."

With that, Tia Rosa put her arms around Mimi and hugged her tight. She told her that she loved her and that they would see her soon. She told Mimi to keep up with her piano. Mimi just nodded and kissed her on the cheek. She turned and walked towards the door, stopping for a moment and turned. She looked around the room trying to memorize everything. Now with tears streaming down her face, she blew her aunt a kiss and stepped outside and got into the care. Tio Javier put her suitcase in the back seat and began the drive to José Marti airport. Tio tried to make light conversation with Mimi. He could tell she was terrified. He could see her bottom lip trembling and her hands shaking. He spent the eighteen mile drive telling her all about the wonderful things she was going to see, and all of the wonderful places she would visit. He re assured her that her father had always loved her, and that he would make sure she was happy.

Mimi sat through the drive quietly. She tried to fight back the tears that were running down her cheeks. She already missed her grandparents, and was now going to miss her Tia and Tio. They had always done so much for her. She missed her friend Antonio, and suddenly realized she didn't remember his last name! How would she ever be able to write to him and let him know where she was? How could she have gone all this time and not known to ask? She loved him, and the thought of never seeing him again made her even sadder.

When they arrived at the airport, Tio parked the car, and they walked quietly towards the front doors. It had only been light outside for a short time. Mimi looked around now that she was able to see, and saw nothing for miles around. Just this big place she had never been to. The soldiers that were guarding the door asked for identification, and visa. Mimi reached inside her small purse and handed them the passport and yellow visa. They looked examined everything closely. They compared the photograph of the young girl, to the now fifteen year old standing in front of them. One of them caught that today was her birthday and made a comment. They asked for Tio to present them with some form of identification, which he did. One of the soldiers motioned them inside the terminal. Once they were inside, they were escorted to an area where there were a lot of children behind a big glass pane. There were two nuns, and a few adults. When they got near, they were asked to say their good byes, and for Mimi to step inside, into the glass room. Mimi turned to look at her uncle and saw tears running down his face.

"Well, this is as far as I can go. Your flight leaves soon and you'll be asked to go get on the airplane. Don't forget where you came from." He said as he gave her a hug. Mimi was overcome with emotion and just nodded her head. She couldn't speak. It was early in the morning, and already she had had the worst day of her life.

As she stepped into the room, she could hear the sound of children and babies crying. She turned to see the families outside of the glass, tearful and devastated. Everyone looked as if they were trying to put on a brave face for the children they were sending away. Sending them with nothing but faith, not knowing if they would ever see them again. Or if they did, how long it would take before they were ever able to hold them or kiss them again.

Suddenly, the door opened. The sound of the spinning propellers could now be heard loud and clear. The adults in the room began to take the small children outside, and walk them onto the tarmac. They handed them to stewardesses and others that were standing waiting at the bottom of the stairs that were propped against the big silver Pan Am airplane ready to take them to their new lives. There was more crying. A woman came and motioned the older children to come outside now. As they were herded towards the door, Mimi looked back and caught a glimpse of her uncle outside the glass, waving. He was holding a handkerchief over his mouth. She feared it might be the last time she would see the lovely kind man.

Mimi reached the bottom of the stairs and looked up. She took a deep breath and climbed the metal stairs and boarded the plane. A stewardess took her to her seat by a window and helped her to put on her seat belt. She could see outside. There was nothing really to look at except those big propellers. Spinning and making a loud noise.

The stewardesses helped place the younger children into their seats. Many of them cried with fear. Some of the older children sat with their baby brothers or sisters on their laps. Everyone looked so unhappy.

After a few minutes, the door to the plane was closed, and after what seemed forever, the plane began to move. The crying and screaming of the younger children got even louder. Most of them calling for their Mothers or

Fathers. Mimi braced herself. She had never flown before.

The airplane seemed to just move for a while, then it began to pick up speed. Before she knew it, they were up in the air. She looked out the window and was amazed to how small cars and houses began to look. The pilot took a route that flew directly over the Havana, just along the coast line. She could see the 'Malecon'. It's a concrete wall that lies just along the water in Havana. She remembered going there in the evenings with her Mom and Dad and just sitting on it, letting the soft evening breeze cool them off. Sometimes, her father would take them to get a milkshake before heading back home. Mimi grew emotional as she saw the crystal clear blue waves hitting the shores of her beloved island. After a few minutes, there was no more land. Just water.

The stewardesses tried to calm everyone by offering them a glass of soda. Mimi took hers and held it in her hands. It helped keep them from shaking as much. She still had a big knot in her throat and didn't think she could swallow it. The flight seemed to take forever. But after about an hour, she saw land again. The plane's landing gear could be heard underneath the plane, locking into place. Objects became bigger again. And then, touchdown. The adults on the airplane broke out in applause and began to shout, "Viva Cuba Libre!" (Long live free Cuba).

When the airplane came to a stop, several men and women came on board and began to take the smaller children and the babies out. Then, everyone else was helped down the stairs and into the Miami Airport terminal. She stepped off the airplane into the unknown. She had no idea of what life had in store for her.

They were all taken to a waiting room. Some of the children were met by family members who had been waiting for them. Others, like Mimi, just sat in another glass room, wondering what was to become of them. A nun brought everyone a bag containing a ham sandwich and a carton of milk. Mimi had never seen bread quite like this. At home, the bread was baked and sliced. This sandwich was made of Wonder Bread, and the milk carton puzzled her. She wasn't quite sure what was in there and how to open it. Her English was rusty, but she understood the word milk. But getting it open was another ordeal. Some of the adults wandering around were helping some of the younger children, so she watched them and was finally able to get to the milk. She was quite hungry now, so she tried to eat the sandwich and drink the milk. She did like the bread. It was soft and chewy.

Several hours passed by. Some of the children were

picked up by relatives throughout the day. Then, the children that were left were put on busses. The boys in one, and the girls into another. Mimi knew no one. She was scared and nervous about where they might end up. When they arrived at their destination, she found herself in a sort of camp for girls. They escorted the girls to different *bunk* buildings. Inside, for the first time, Mimi saw bunk beds. Six on one side of the room, and six on the other. There were four girls including her, taken to the one she'd been assigned to. There were already eight girls who had apparently been taken there some time before them. There was someone there from just about every age group. The youngest seemed to be about five. She and her sister, who looked to be around twelve or thirteen, had been on the airplane that morning. The girls that were there, laid on their beds, or stood around staring at the new arrivals. Mimi didn't know what to do. She saw the other girls take their suitcases and put them on a bed. So she decided to do the same. A couple of the girls who weren't new, started talking to them. Asking their names and where they were from. Several of them were telling the new girls about the routine at the camp. Everyone got up at seven, washed in commune showers, got dressed and went to the cafeteria after they made their beds. They had to do their own laundry and make sure the bunk room was kept clean. They all helped out cleaning the bathrooms as well. This horrified Mimi. She's never cleaned a thing in her life. And as for laundry, she had no clue as to how that was done. Listening to these girls made her longue for the plantation, and she missed everyone there.

When the afternoon came, they all walked into the dining room to have their evening meal. She followed everyone and did as they did. Everyone stood in a single line and took a tray. They slid it down as the ladies behind the counter scooped food and plopped it onto plates that they put on the trays. Mimi remembered the tales of the Automats. But this wasn't quite what she had in mind. The food didn't look very tasty. It was a piece of chicken, mashed potatoes with gravy, which she'd never had in her life. Another carton of milk, and an apple. Everyone sat on long tables and visited with one another as they ate. Still in kind of shock, Mimi sat alone at the end of one of the tables. As she played with her food, another girl came and sat across from her. She introduced herself as Dolores.

"How old are you and where are you from?" She asked Mimi.

"I'm fifteen today. I grew up mostly in Pinar del Rio. Where are you from?"

"Havana. I'm sixteen. I've been here for a whole

week already. I don't know where I'll end up. I was talking to one of the Sisters the other day. They are trying to place me in a home. I have no relatives here in America. My Abuela put me on the plane. I really miss her. How about you? Is someone coming after you?

"My father. I'm supposed to give an envelope with his address to anyone who will help me so they can let him know I'm here. He'll come and get me."

"You're lucky." Said Dolores. "I have no idea who is going to take care of me. I don't even speak English."

"I speak English. My father is American. I had a tutor."

"Oh, you're one of those spoiled rich ones. Be careful. A couple of the older girls in our room are very mean. They'll pick on you if you give them reason to. Tomorrow, I'll take you to go see Sister Barbara Mary. She's nice. She'll help you find your father. Don't you like the food?"

"What is this?" Asked Mimi pointing to the mashed potatoes.

"I think its potatoes. They smash them in America and they look like that. The brown stuff on top I don't know what it is. But it isn't bad. You'll get used to it. Hurry up. We're going to have to go back to our rooms soon. They turn the lights out right at nine."

Mimi played with her food some more, and managed to eat some of the chicken. After everyone was finished, all the girls went outside. Some of them were jumping rope. Others were using the swings. The older ones just stood around in groups talking. Mimi walked around for a bit before sitting on a bench. She just sat there wondering what was to become of her. It was her fifteenth birthday. This wasn't the way she had envisioned spending it. She wondered how her grandparents were. She missed Antonio and hated that she'd been rushed away before she had a chance to say good bye to him. Little did she know, that when her uncle got back to the house, there had been news telling her Tia and Tio of the fate her grandparents had met. And Antonio had no idea what had happened to Mimi.

At around eight thirty, everyone was told to get inside and change their clothes. They were going to have to get ready for bed. Mimi wandered inside the bunk room and watched as the girls all put on their pajamas. She knew there was a pair in her suitcase, but had never had to put them on alone. Someone one had always helped dress her. And they had brushed her beautiful hair. A few minutes before nine, one of the older girls asked her,

"Hey, aren't you going to get changed? You have to go to bed now. Get those clothes off and change into your sleeping clothes."

"I don't know how to get this off." She said as she pointed to the zipper on the back side of her dress."

Everyone broke into laughter. From the smallest to the oldest. They were all laughing at her. She felt humiliated as she stood there turning red.

"Aw, look at the Princess." Said one of the older girls laughing and pointing at her. "Her Highness doesn't know how to work a zipper. We're going to call you Princess. The 'Peter Pan Princess'!" Everyone began to laugh.

This was all Mimi could take for one day. She began to sob letting it all out as they continued to laugh at her. Then the lights went out. Everyone got into their beds and the mean girls continued to laugh as she stood there still fully clothed. She finally got into her bed and pulled the covers over her head. Many of the smaller girls cried for their Mama. She cried too for hours, finally drifting off to sleep late into the night. It had been a very long and very tiring few days for her.

Chapter 9

Early in the morning, Dolores shook Mimi awake. She helped her out of bed and gave her a hand removing her dress before the others got up. She told her to pick out clothes and helped her get into them.

"After breakfast, I'm going to take you to see Sister Barbara Mary. She'll know what to do with the envelope you have. She's very nice, you'll see."

It was Mimi's first introduction to cereal that morning. The food in America was different. And after enduring more of the taunting by the older girls in the cafeteria, calling her by her new nick name, Dolores took Mimi into the office where two of the Sisters that overlooked the camp were. There she met Sister Patrice, and Sister Barbara Mary. .

"Sister Barbara, this is my new friend Mimi. She has an envelope with her American father's name in it. Can you help her find him?"

Sister Barbara Mary spoke perfect Spanish. She was a tall thin woman that looked to be in her middle fifties, with kind brown eyes. Her hair tucked under her head cover. She wore a dark navy blue dress that hit just below her knees. Hanging from a chain around her, neck was a pair of large black glasses with very thick lenses. She lifted them and placed them on the end of her nose. She then took a long look at Mimi and began thumbing through some papers on her desk.

"Are you Maribel Bennis Morales?" She asked in her near perfect Spanish.

"Yes I am. I'm Maribel. But everyone calls me Mimi. My mother gave me that nick name."

"I was getting ready to come looking for you. I'm sorry I didn't have time to get to your yesterday. It was very busy day with many arrivals. We had twelve babies and we were shorthanded. One of our sisters wasn't feeling well and she didn't want to pass whatever she has to any of you children. I understand your father lives here is America. Somewhere here in Florida?"

"I don't know where, but my aunt gave me this envelope with an address in it. Please can you find him and tell him to come and pick me up? I want to go home with my father."

Mimi handed her the envelope. Sister Barba opened it and pulled out a paper with some writing. It had Robert Bennis's name and an address but no telephone.

"There is no way of calling your father." She said with a disappointed sound to her voice. "There is no telephone number written here. But I'll do my best to find him for you. You just have to be patient. Where is your Mother? Is she still in Cuba?"

"My Mother is dead Sister. She died when I was very little. I only have one parent now."

"I'll see if I can get a number from the telephone book to call him. If not, I'll have to take a bus to where he lives and let him know you are here. As you can see, there are many children in our care. This might take me some time. So many children need to be placed. But I'll do my very best to find your father as quickly as I can. In the meantime, try to enjoy your time here and make new friends."

"Oh thank you sister. I know he wouldn't want me here any longer than necessary. He'll come and get me you'll see."

"Yes, well, just be patient. We really have our work cut out for us here with everyone we're trying to help. It might take a few days if his phone number isn't listed in the book. I'll do the best I can. Dolores, you'll help watch out for her won't you? I'm working on placing you with a nice family as well."

"Thank you Sister. Mimi and I are going to be best friends you'll see. Come Mimi, let's go back to the playground."

Dolores took Mimi by the hand and they walked outside. As they walked towards the play area, Dolores noticed that her new friend had begun to cry again. She told her that she had to have faith and that everyone will end up where they were supposed to until they were with their families again. She tried to distract Mimi by asking her to tell her all about her family and where she grew up. Sitting on a bench, they began to share stories and finally managed to get one another to laugh. At least for a while. Dolores told Mimi her story. She had no family here in America. Her Grandmother had put her on the Peter Pan flight alone because she was too old and too sick to travel. Her Mother and father were *Fidelistas*, and had abandoned her as a newborn. Her grandmother was all the family she'd ever had, as her parents had gone off to join in the 'regime'. They felt Dolores would only get in their way.

"My *Abuela* knew she couldn't take care of me for too much longer and wanted a better life for me than what she said was coming for Cuba. I know I'll never see her again. But I'm going to write to her as much as I can. We knew when we said goodbye that it would be our last hug. But she loved me enough to make that sacrifice. I know it took all she had to put me on that airplane. Sister Barbara Mary is looking for a foster home for me here where I can live with a new family."

"I'm sorry for you Dolores. At least I know I have my Father here and he'll come and get me. Maybe I can ask him if you can come to live with us too."

"I'd really like that! We can be Peter Pan Sisters!"

They both giggled and decided to go for a walk around the camp and explore. As they came around the front of the property near the office where the Sisters worked, they noticed a small white chapel. They saw that the door and windows were open. They looked through the windows. It looked like someone had been inside cleaning.

"Look, there is a piano in there. Let's go inside. I should practice. My Abuela would be very happy if she knew I didn't abandon my lessons just because I came to America."

The girls stepped into the small white chapel, and as is the Catholic tradition, dipped their fingers in the Holy Water and made the sign of the cross. The chapel had a beautiful stained glass window behind the altar and a simple cross with Jesus in front. It held only about twelve rows of pews. To the left of the altar was the piano.

"Do you think we'll get into trouble if you play it?" Asked Dolores.

"I don't see why. There isn't a sign that says I can't. And if they don't like it, they'll come and tell me to stop. I'll stop then."

Dolores sat on one of the pews in the front, while her friend walked over to the beautiful white piano and raised the cover over the keys. She watched as Mimi took a seat on the bench and ran her hands over the cold ivory keys as if she were enthralled by their feel. A grin came over her face. Mimi closed her eyes and sat for a moment as if she was clearing her mind of everything. Then, she positioned her hands on the keys, took a deep breath and began to play. The song was one familiar to every Cuban patriot, as what she had elected to play was The Cuban National Anthem: 'La Bayamesa.' Her command of the piano was strong and precise. Every note played with intent and emotion.

Dolores didn't know if she should kneel of stand? After all, she *was* in a church.

Before Mimi finished her long version of the anthem, the two Sisters had dashed in to see who it was playing the piano with such perfection. Everyone nearby also rushed over to see who it was, as well as many of the children from the playground who had heard the music, now stood outside the windows and looking in.

When she finished, everyone applauded. They shouted "Bravo!" Sister Barbara Mary looked stunned. Dolores didn't know what to say or what to think. Her new friend had a beautiful talent.

"Mimi!" Said Sister Barbara with great enthusiasm. "That was simply amazing!" Where did you learn to play the piano like that? Why, you are quite the virtuoso."

"I learned to play first from my Mother when I was very little. She used to put me on her lap with my hands on hers and we would play the piano together all the time. Then I took lessons until I came here to America. I've been playing all of my life."

"Well, I think it might be a good idea for you to keep up with your practices during your time here with us. We wouldn't want to you to get rusty. Feel free to come in and play during the day when you want. Maybe you can entertain some of the other children and they can sing along or something."

"Thank you Sister." Said Mimi. "I'll do that. It would make the time go faster for me."

"Play something else!" Shouted someone from the window.

"Yes Mimi, play something else." Said Dolores with a big smile on her face.

Mimi put her hands on the keyboard and again began to play. This time, it was the soft soothing melody from the Nutcracker. Tchaikovsky's "The Dance of the Sugar Plumb Fairy". The Sisters stood in the back of the chapel and watched for some time. They were genuinely happy to hear such lovely music being made by such a young girl. They agreed she had great promise. Dolores sat moving her foot to the music. More and more of the kids came to hear her play. Some came inside out of the heat and took a seat on the pews or on the floor along the walls to listen to her play. Even some of the mean girls stood outside and watched as she played. She entertained everyone for the afternoon and everyone seemed to like it.

At that moment, Sister Barbara Mary knew she had to do what she could to find Mimi's father soon. Such a talented girl deserved to be home with her family.

That night before lights out, everyone said their good nights to the 'Peter Pan Princess'. But this time it wasn't said with ridicule. It was with admiration and affection. Her nick name was now easier for Mimi to handle knowing she was being accepted instead of rejected because of her privileged upbringing.

Chapter 10

Sister Barbara Mary stepped off a bus at a corner on to the main street that leads into Miami Beach, Julia Tuttle Causeway. She held in her hand a piece of paper that had an address she had been given by Mimi. Not knowing if this was still the correct address or not, she knew this was a mission she had to take. She said a prayer and hoped she was headed in the right direction. If not, she prayed it would at least be a starting place.

Walking down the street, she noticed a lot of the businesses and offices had the Star of David in the windows and a Mezuzah on the door post. This indicated the business office or home of someone of the Jewish faith. Looking up at the addresses and down at her paper, she traveled about three blocks until she found the number by the door that matched. The sign above the door said "Accountant". She knew she was at the right *address*. Now, she had to find out if she had found the right *place*.

Opening the door slowly, she heard the sound of a tiny a bell. She stood in the entrance inside the door and didn't see anyone. But knew the bell would alarm someone of her arrival. Looking around the room, she saw a very humble office with an oak desk and a lamp on top. A telephone and stacks of papers. Nothing fancy but clean. Not long after, a man in his early thirties appeared from behind a black curtain that hid a door opening. He was a very attractive man with a well-trimmed beard that matched his hair, and payots, or side locks. Payots were the long side burns worn in a curl on both sides of his face, as is a tradition for some men of the Jewish faith. And he wore a yamaka on the crown of his head. He seemed startled to see a Catholic Nun standing at his door and was suddenly taken back.

"May I help you Sister?" he said with a puzzled look on his face. "Are you lost?"

"I'm not sure." She said as she looked into his eyes. "I'm looking for Robert Bennis. Do you know where I might find him?"

"Well Sister, you have found him. How can I help you?" he asked in a soft voice.

Sister Barbara Mary looked around the room and noticed several other men coming out of the back, also looking stunned at the sight of a nun in their lobby. "Is there some place we can talk in private?" She asked not wanting to address her needs in front of anyone else.

"Please follow me. We can go in my office."

Robert led Sister Barbara behind the dark curtain down

a long hall to a steep set of stairs. She followed him up and inside the first door on the left.

"Please sit down and tell me what this is all about."

Robert motioned her to take a seat on chair across his desk and he took the seat facing her. The office was small and cramped. There were filing cabinets everywhere. Several adding machines were on his desk and there were jars full of pencils. On the wall behind him was a picture of a Rabbi.

"Mr. Bennis, I'll get right to it. I'm sure you're a very busy man. I don't know if you've heard of the Peter Pan flights from Havana to Miami? Children are being sent by their families to other relatives or friends here in America in the hopes of sparing them from the Castro Regime and revolution that is taking place in Cuba. I am one of the care givers the Catholic Church has assigned to assist in reuniting these children with their families, or placing them in foster homes until their families can come to claim them. One of the children that arrived recently gave me a piece of paper with your name on it. It says that you're her father. Her name is Maribel Bennis. She is called 'Mimi' for short."

Sister Barbara watched as the color drained out of Robert's face. He sat back in his chair and slumped. He shook his head in disbelief. Tears began to roll down his face and he seemed unable to speak.

"Mr. Bennis are you all right?" She asked with a concerned look on her face.

It took Robert a couple of minutes to gather himself. He took a handkerchief out of his back pocket, wiped his tears and blew his nose. After clearing his throat, he addressed Sister Barbara.

"I have a daughter by that name. I left Cuba with my parents sometime after her mother was accidently killed. Her death is something I've never been able to recover from. But my parents were elderly and the revolutionists were starting to persecute my people. I brought them here because I had to look after them. Mimi was left in the care of her Grandparents. I've not been able to contact them by telephone for over a year now. I was afraid they had all perished. All of the news we hear from the radio broadcasts is telling us that Castro's men are killing business men and property owners and stealing everyone's land and homes. I thought they were all dead."

"Well, your daughter is very much alive. She's a beautiful young girl with a talent for the piano like none I have ever seen or heard. She needs to come home and be with her family. When can you come and pick her up?"

Robert lowered his head had to wipe his face again. The tears had begun to flow down his face once again.

"I'm not sure that I can. You see, I have remarried and we have two young boys. My wife knows about Sara, Mimi's mother. But she forbids me to speak of her. I'm going to have to give some thought to this and how to handle this. I'll need some time."

"I understand your situation Mr. Bennis. But this is your child. Won't you please at least come to see her this week, say, Thursday afternoon? This will give you some time to discuss this with your wife and family. I won't say anything to Mimi just yet. It would be wonderful if you could surprise her. Here is the address where we are. I'll look forward to your visit later this week."

Sister Barbara handed Robert a piece of paper with her name, and the address to the camp. She stood, shook his hand and made her way out of his office, and down the steep stairs. Robert followed her but didn't speak. As she stepped outside, she saw at a distance that her bus coming down the street, and hurried to catch it. She took a seat and watched as the doors closed. Content that she had been able to find Mimi's father, she wondered why she had such a bad feeling in her stomach. Something just didn't seem right. She pulled out her rosary beads and decided to pray about it and ask God for guidance.

Chapter 11

Mimi sat at the piano Thursday afternoon during a small rain storm. Her music seemed to reflect her mood. The week before, her friend Dolores had been placed with a nice Catholic family. Their home was not too far from the high school she'd be attending later in the month when school started. The Rodriguez family had a daughter in Junior High School. Mimi was there to support her friend when they came by, for the meeting between Dolores and the family. They were kind and humble Cuban people that had been in the United States now for seven years. They had a small three bedroom house in Hialeah. He was a baker and she stayed home. They had never been able to have more children and their daughter Carla had always wanted a sister. Being members of the church that sponsored the Peter Pan children in the area, they had decided to take in one of the girls that didn't have any family in the United States and give her a home. Mimi had gone to their house along with Dolores and Sister Barbara earlier that week to drop Dolores off at her the Rodriguez house, near the camp where they were now. They had prepared a room for her next to their daughter's bedroom. It was small, but nice and clean. They visited for about two hours and had to say good bye. The girls hugged one another and promised to stay in touch. Mrs. Rodriguez gave Mimi their telephone number and said she could come over to visit any time she wanted to.

Now, alone in a new country, her only friend had moved on. She played soft quiet music listening to the sound of the rain, and wondered when she would be going home with her Father. She knew they were trying to locate him. But in the meantime, more children came and went. Others that were there when she arrived had gone. She had begun to feel anxious.

At around three in the afternoon, Robert Bennis walked into Sister Barbara Mary's office. He shook his umbrella outside the door and left it as not to wet the floor inside. Sister Barbara stood to greet him and shook his hand.

"Well, you must be anxious to reunite with your daughter. Why don't I send for her?" She said as she smiled and looked into his eyes. But what she saw wasn't the look of a parent ready to see his child. She knew that the gut feeling she'd had when she left him earlier in the week was right.

"Mr. Bennis, why don't you come inside my office so we can talk?" She said as she turned and led him inside. She closed the door behind him and sat on the chair across from him. She could tell he was troubled. His hands trembled. His bottom lip quivered as he gathered the strength to speak. Clearing his throat, he looked up and said, "I can't take Mimi home with me Sister. I'm sorry. I wish I could but it's just not possible."

"Mr. Bennis, you don't understand. You are the only family this young girl has now. She is alone in a new country without anyone to love and care for her. You need to step up and do the right thing. She's your blood! Her family has entrusted you to be her parent and take care of her. There is no one else and we can't send her back!"

"I've spoken to my wife about the situation. You see, Mimi is an identical replica of her mother. It would be like seeing Sara every time I looked at her. I could never be able to move forward with my life. I promised my new young wife when we married, that, that part of my life was behind me. I gave her my word never to speak of Sara. In my religion, that wasn't a marriage in the eyes of God. She was not of the Jewish faith. It was a marriage that was doomed from the start. But we loved one another so much, our families agreed to it rather than alienate us. I've now become closer to God and pray every day for my atonement. My wife feels that if I bring Mimi into our lives, *our* marriage will be doomed as well, and she fears for the lives of our two sons."

Sister Barbara Mary looked at Robert and understood his pleading, but lowered her head and shook it in disappointment. She knew it wasn't her place to judge him, but feared for Mimi.

"What is to become of the child?" She asked as her face filled with emotion and despair. Robert had no answer for her.

Instead, he pulled an envelope containing money from the inside pocket of his black jacked and placed it in Sister Barbara's hands. "Please, use this to help her. It's all I can do. I'll sign adoption papers if you find her a good home. But she just can't be part of my life. I love her more than you could ever know. But I don't have it inside of me to bring her back into my life. It would be too painful. It just can't happen. I'm sorry, but it just can't happen."

"At least see the child. I know you haven't seen her in many years. She is grown into such a beautiful person. Please let me take you to her. She doesn't have to know you are here. She's playing the piano in the Chapel. You can look at her and listen to her play." Pleated Sister Barbara Mary.

Reluctantly Robert followed her. As they got closer, he could hear the music coming from the inside. It was stirring memories he hadn't felt in a very long time. As he approached the entrance to the Chapel, he paused and stood near the door looking through the glass. He could see her from the side as she played. Her long hair draped down her back, and the concentration on her face as she touched the ivory keys moved him to tears once again. The expression on her face, and the way she moved around the keyboard was uncanny. It was as if he were watching Sara once again. Afraid she would spot him, he turned and hurried off. Sister Barbara could hear him as he wept loudly on the way to his car.

What was she going to say to Mimi? She couldn't lie to her. She'd have to find the way to break it to her. She wouldn't be able to go home to her Father's house. Somehow, the frail sad nun would have to find a place to send her to. But she was determined to find her a home.

Later that evening after supper, she sent for Mimi and asked her to walk with her so they could talk. Sister Barbara Mary took Mimi across the street to the park and they sat on a bench while she broke the news to her. She tried to be strong for the young girl but knew she was breaking her heart. Mimi cried and shouted in disbelief. Holding her as she wept, it brought her to tears as well. Mimi had loved her Daddy, and the thought of his rejection was more than she thought she could bare. Her

Mother was dead, her Grandparents and her Aunt and Uncle were across the ocean in another country. Who knew if she would ever see them again? But Sister Barbara assured her that she would try to place her in a nice home and try to find a family to adopt her. She told her it would be her mission to do so.

"You will be something great someday, I know it. This is America. Anything is possible in America. Have faith child." She said to the young girl as she watched her crumble before her. But that wasn't what Mimi had wanted to hear at that moment. She wanted to hear that she would finally be leaving for her new home. She felt alone in the world with no one to love her or take care of her. She wondered what was to become of her.

Mimi cried herself to sleep that night. Some of the kids asked, "What's the matter Princess?" But she didn't respond. She felt ashamed and alone. So very much alone.

Chapter 12

As the days passed, Sister Barbara Mary spent many hours on the telephone calling parishioners, and other parish offices trying to find someone that would be willing to give Mimi a home. Determined to place her before the school year began, she located a priest at one of the nearby parishes who had mentioned a Cuban family in his church that was having a tough time making ends meet. So she called him. Sister Barbara hadn't spoken to anyone of the two thousand dollars Robert had brought to help care for Mimi. She discussed this with him and he thought this family might be willing to take her in if there was something in it for them. It would be a win-win situation. They would get a little money until the husband could find work again, and Mimi would have a place to stay. Perhaps on a permanent basis if things worked out. If not, at least it would temporarily get her out of the camp and into a family home. But she hoped it would work out, and make it a permanent situation. If not, it would get Mimi out of the camp, and that family would have help paying some of the bills and buying food. Sister Barbara called Mimi to her office and told her of her plan. She told

Mimi then about the money her father had left for her and she agreed to give it a try.

Father Murphy arranged the meeting between the family, Sister Barbara and Mimi. They drove to the house after dinner one evening. It wasn't the greatest neighborhood, but the house was neat and tidy. Mrs. Ramirez greeted them at the door. She was a short very stocky woman in her late thirties who was as wide as she was tall. She had short jet black hair combed straight back and had a plastic headband holding it in place. Mr. Ramirez was not too much taller and not much thinner. Balding on the top, he too had jet black hair with some kind of shinny hair jell all over it. He was wearing a wife beater that was stained with coffee that he had spilled down the front, and had a toothpick in his mouth. There were two young boys in the house sitting on the plastic covered gold velour sofa. They looked to be about eight and nine years old. There were pictures and statues of Saints cluttering just about every nook and cranny in the living room, and a very large picture of Jesus hung above the sofa. Red velour curtains adorned the windows. They looked as if they hadn't been dusted forever. There was no air conditioning but they had a big square metal fan sitting on a chair blowing full blast.

Father Murphy, Sister Barbara and Mimi were asked to

take a seat on the sofa and the boys were sent to their room. The conversation began introducing everyone. It seemed Mr. Ramirez was a truck driver who had lost his job after he'd had an accident that resulted in his company being sued due to his alcohol level. Mrs. Ramirez did all of the talking. Mr. Ramirez just sat on a chair and looked at Mimi while his toothpick moved from one side of his mouth to the other. He was supposed to be actively looking for work but had experienced a bit of bad luck due to his circumstance. Mrs. Ramirez was taking in laundry, and ironing from the neighborhood to help put food on the table.

Mimi was very uncomfortable sitting in the tiny living room. She knew she was going to have to leave the camp, but had never pictured herself in such living conditions. Her life style had been so different in Cuba. The opulent spacious homes with large elegant rooms and servants were now a thing of her past. It was hard to grasp what her life would be like from now on. She felt anger at having nothing a say about the direction it was taking. Everyone said they had her best interest in mind. But looking around, it didn't seem that way at all. She longed for her family and her home. She longed for the luscious green farm and her piano and ballet lessons. She missed her island country. But most of all, she missed her Abuela combing her hair at night while the cool island breeze softly entered her bedroom. And the promise of a different life now gone because of a communist dictator who had come to selfishly ruin the lives of so many.

The tiny house had only two bedrooms. One of them was shared by the boys. But Mrs. Ramirez showed Mimi and Sister Barbara a laundry room off of the kitchen where they had put a cot in for Mimi to sleep and a small night stand that had two drawers where she could keep some of her things. The sight of this brought Mimi to tears. But she hid them from everyone. She turned her head and walked back to the living room as she wiped them away. This was to be her life now and she had to accept it. It certainly wasn't like the picture books she had back home. This wasn't her vision of America at all.

"Well it's settled then. Mimi and I will pack her things tomorrow and I will drop her off in the afternoon. It was very nice meeting you both." Said Sister Barbara as she shook hands and motioned Mimi and Father Murphy to the door. Once inside the car, Sister Barbara asked Mimi if she was all right.

"You are very quiet my dear. Is something the matter?" She asked with a concerned look on her face.

"Sister, I didn't get a good feeling in there. I don't think I can go there to live."

"Well, you really have no alternative at this point. I've been searching for weeks to find you a home and I'm afraid I have exhausted all of my ability. We are trying to help so many other children and your situation has taken up a lot of my time. I'm afraid it's the best I can do. Why don't we give it a try for a bit and see how things go. Who knows, you might like the Ramirez family and they might want to adopt you. They only have two boys. And it's walking distance from the high school. You can join the music program there and continue with your piano. Let's just see how it goes. I won't forget you. I'll check in on you soon."

The following afternoon, Mimi said her good byes to the girls in her room at the camp and went off to her new home. Mrs. Ramirez met them at the door and Sister Barbara Mary handed Mimi's suitcase to her. Mimi turned and hugged Sister Barbara really tight.

"I won't come in. I'll leave you two now to get to know one another." She handed Mrs. Ramirez an envelope and waved at them. Mrs. Ramirez told Mimi to come into the kitchen and to put her things in her room. Mimi walked into the tiny laundry room and placed what she could inside of the drawers. She didn't really have much, but the few things that didn't fit she left in the suitcase and slid it under the bed. Mrs. Ramirez was cooking in the kitchen and Mimi stood watching from the door.

"Now you know you'll have to help around her just like everyone else. I know you are used to having servants. But there's no servants here. I'll find things for you to do. We only have one bathroom and I like it cleaned every day. That can be your job starting tomorrow. I'll show you where everything is to clean." She said this to Mimi while giving her a snarly look. Mimi was horrified! Clean a bathroom? She'd never cleaned anything much less a bathroom. She wouldn't know what to do? Where to start. This wasn't starting in a good place all ready.

"In the drawer over in that cabinet are the tablecloth and the napkins. Take them over to the table and set it."

Mimi had never set a table but had watched her Tia and the servants do it. There didn't seem to be much to it, so she gave it a try. She placed the dishes that were on the counter in front of every chair, and remembered where to put the knife and forks. When she finished, she smiled and told herself. *I can do this. I can live like a regular person.*

Shortly after she was done, Mr. Ramirez walked in the door with the two boys. He went into the bedroom without so much as saying a word to his wife or Mimi.

He was wearing the same dirty T-shirt he had on the day before. The two boys went into the kitchen to ask what was for dinner. They looked shyly at Mimi and asked her if she liked to read. Mimi asked them if they had any books and they offered to show her. She followed them into their tiny room that held two twin beds side by side with barely enough room to walk between them. The younger one said his name was Oscar and pointed at the older one. "That's Tomas." He said, reaching under his bed. He brought out some comic books and showed them to Mimi. Tomas asked Mimi if she would read one to them and she began looking through to select one, just as Mrs. Ramirez called everyone to the table.

"You sit over there." She instructed Mimi as she pointed to a chair beside Oscar. Mr. Ramirez came and sat at the head of the table and Mrs. Ramirez and Tomas to his right. Mrs. Ramirez began to scoop the rice and black beans onto everyone's plates. Then she passed around a dish with some fried chicken she had just finished preparing. No one was saying very much, and Mimi was afraid to say anything since she really didn't know much about anyone. Mr. Ramirez finally opened the conversation directing it at Mimi.

"So, we hear you came from Pinar del Rio from a tobacco farm. What was the name?"

"La Sonrisa. My family has worked the land for several generations."

"So you people had some money huh? We came from Camaguey. You ever been to there?"

"Yes. I've been there with my Grandmother several times."

"Reynaldo, don't talk so much and eat your dinner before it gets cold." Said Mrs. Ramirez looking sternly at her husband. No one else said anything for the duration of the meal. When they were done, the boys ran outside the door to play without clearing their plates. It was hot and very uncomfortable in the house. Mr. Ramirez went to sit in the living room and turned on the television. Mrs. Ramirez signaled Mimi to help clear off the plates and bring them into the kitchen.

"I think I'm going to visit my neighbor next door. You do the dishes since I cooked. Have them done when I get back."

She turned and went out the back door, lit a cigarette and walked away. Mimi looked stunned. Wash dishes? She'd never washed dishes. She didn't know where to begin.

Looking around the kitchen, she noticed a small pan in the sink with water in it, and rag and a white soap that smelled awful. She began to rinse the plates under the running water and used the rag in the pan to wipe them. As she did this, she felt her eyes fill with tears. Her face turned red and she began to cry. She was angry and hurt. Right then she knew they were going to use her more like a servant that a member of the family. This woman was mean. She was mean to her husband and to her children. And now she was going to be mean to her.

When Mimi finished the dishes, she could feel the sweat dripping down her back. Having accomplished what she initially thought might have been an impossible task, she decided to walk out the screen door that led from the kitchen onto the back porch. She took a seat on the top step and took a deep breath. It was dark now, and the stars were coming out. She began to feel the slight breeze blowing through the nearby trees that began to cool her and she was grateful. In the darkness, she could see the stars in the sky and remembered sitting under them with Antonio. She wondered if he were outside now, could he be looking at the same stars? She hoped he missed her as much as she missed him. She waited to see a falling star so she could make a wish for her old life back. But it wasn't to be. Not that night. Suddenly she heard Mrs. Ramirez burst through the front door with both of the boys, yelling at them to go to bed. Mimi decided she too would go to bed in her little room too. She wanted to go to sleep so she could forget about where she was. At least while she was sleeping, she didn't have to think about the hell her life was turning into.

Chapter 13

On the first day of school, Mimi didn't know what to expect. Having been privately tutored all of her life, this was to be a new experience for her.

During the orientation she and Mrs. Ramirez had attended the Friday before, she'd been given a schedule and had taken a tour of the classrooms she would be attending for this semester. The school bus was a whole new experience in itself. She didn't know anyone, and no one spoke to her. Everyone seemed to speak in English. And she was a bit out of practice. She understood *some* words, but it seemed to her that everyone spoke too fast for her to clearly understand. With map in hand, she managed to find her Home Room. There she took a seat and heard the first school bell ever. The unexpected sound made her jump and several of the students that saw it, laughed at her.

The first few hours spent in that class consisted of filling out forms. This overwhelmed Mimi. Mrs. Sears her Home Room teacher noticed her struggling and approached her to see if she needed help. She spoke some Spanish and between the two of them, managed to communicate and get them completed. Mrs. Sears assured her that things would get easier with each day and showed Mimi much appreciated kindness.

At the sound of the second bell, everyone seemed to run out the door to their next class. Mimi was terrified walking the halls. The school seemed so big to her! She felt like everyone was staring at her. People were bumping into her from all directions.

By the end of the second period, she saw everyone heading to the center of the campus and watched as they opened their lunch bags or purchased food to eat. Mimi took a seat at the end of a picnic table under a large tree and opened a brown paper bag Mrs. Ramirez had given her. Inside, she found a sandwich with some kind of brown spread she'd never seen before. She took her first bite, and spit it out! "Yuk!" She exclaimed out loud. One of the three other girls sitting at the other end of the table noticed her, and scooted down to speak to her.

"You're new aren't you?" She asked. Mimi understood her and replied.

"Yes, I'm from Cuba."

"Oh, are you one of those kids that came alone on a plane or are you here with your family?"

"No, I am alone. My family is still there."

"Don't you like Peanut butter?" Asked the young girl? "That's Peanut butter in there." She said as she pointed to the sandwich.

"I have never eat this before. I no like very much." Said Mimi in English with her Spanish accent.

The young girl reached over to her brown bag and pulled out a banana and gave it to Mimi.

"You'll get used to it. Here in America we eat that for lunch a lot. Here, have a banana. Well, have a good day."

With that, the young girl scooted back to her friends. Mimi heard her talking to them but she couldn't hear what they were saying. They all looked in her direction, smiled and went about their conversation.

When the bell rang indicating lunch time was over, Mimi collected her books and map. As she began to make her way to the next class, she noticed a group of kids towards the end of the cafeteria area and suddenly heard one call out to her in Spanish…..

"Hey! There she is! The Peter Pan Princess! Hello your highness!" They began pointing, laughing and whistling at her.

Two of the *mean girls* from the camp were there and began mocking her in front of the other students. They were obviously attending school there and had formed a group with some of the other Cuban kids on campus.

Mimi was horrified! The last thing she needed was to be made fun of at school. She already felt like an outsider and was very self-conscious. She just wanted the ground to open and swallow her up right then and there. And as if it couldn't get any worse, a couple of them were in her afternoon classes. One of the boys sat behind her in the math class and blew on the back of her neck for the entire class. But being afraid of retribution, she said nothing to the teacher.

At the end of the day, Mimi found herself in a music class. There she found refuge in something she knew she would be good at. There was very little language barrier through music. The teacher, Mrs. Shear, passed out several instruments to the students and asked if anyone played the piano. Mimi and one other girl raised their hands. The teacher asked the other girl to come down and play something for her so she could distinguish the level at which she played. It was nice, but not without mistakes.

Then it was Mimi's turn to play. As she sat at the keys, she felt as she had found her only friend in the world. The keys were her refuge. They were her safe haven. When she began to play, everyone in the class stopped talking. The teacher and the other piano student were stunned at the mastery of her talent.

When she finished, everyone applauded and some of the students even whistled. The teacher asked to see Mimi after class. So she stayed. When everyone had left, Mrs.

Shear took a seat on the chair next to Mimi.

"You're one of the new Cuban students?" She asked smiling at Mimi.

"Yes, I'm new to America. I've always wanted to come to live here. But not in this way."

"Where did you learn to play? How long have you been playing?"

"I learned with my Mother when I was little. But then I had a teacher that came to my house. Until I came to live here. Now I don't have a piano where I live. I'm happy to come to this class and play now." Said Mimi struggling with her English.

"Well, I have to say, you have talent that is beyond this class. I'm not quite sure what to do with you other than just have you stay after school and let you practice so you don't forget your piano skills. Would you like to do that?"

"Oh yes! Very much. Thank you. But I will miss the bus. The house I live at is very far to walk."

"Well, perhaps I can drive you home on the days and let you stay. Will that be alight with the family you are staying with?"

"I don't know. I've only been there one week. I don't know them very good. I have to clean the bathroom."

"Well….how about I take you home today, and we'll ask? That way we can figure out which days you can stay or which ones you might need to go home. Would you like me to do that?"

A smile came over Mimi's face. Finally something good had come of her day. "Yes, I would like that very much. Thank you, thank you!"

So for the next couple of months. Mimi was allowed to stay with Mrs. Shear on Tuesdays and Wednesday afternoons for a couple of hours. It was the only refuge she had. She felt safe there, and playing the piano transported her to another place. She didn't have to think about her life in the Ramirez house, which had been deteriorating since she got there. And how miserable she was at school with the taunting she had to take from the refugee camp girls.

Mimi had confided in Mrs. Shear, that Mr. Ramirez still hadn't found a job, and that he'd been coming home in the middle of the night stumbling in the door. He and Mrs. Ramirez had awful arguments that would sometimes last for over an hour. He'd sometimes sneak into the house through the kitchen door, and she could see him starring through the darkness into the small room where she slept. It made Mimi very uncomfortable. In fact, she had caught him staring at her during dinner, or at odd times in the evening. Especially when she'd sit at the dining room table to study. He would glare at her from his chair in the living room while he pretended to watch television when Mrs. Ramirez was next door visiting with the neighbors. She visited with them every evening. Mimi figured it was her way of not having to deal with him when he was home. Mr. Ramirez had started going out drinking late at night after his wife put the boys to bed. He would start an argument and slam the door. Mimi wondered where he was getting the money since he had no job. She wondered if it was the money Mrs. Ramirez was supposed to be holding for *her* in case she needed anything, or to help buy food. There were times, Mrs. Ramirez would give the boys a steak for dinner and only give Mimi fried eggs. Certainly none of it had been used to buy her anything, and she was still having to get used to the taste of *Peanut butter*!

Chapter 14

Mimi had heard the kids at school talking about the upcoming long weekend, and of a celebration she had never heard of: *Thanksgiving.* She dreaded having to spend all that time at the Ramirez house. School was where she would go the escape her life there. She'd started to get friendly with some of the girls in her homeroom, who were fascinated listening to her talk about her life in Cuba. Things were so different here. The opulence of Mimi's life was something these girls could only imagine. And Mimi looked forward to the days she stayed after school to practice her piano with Mrs. Shear. Now, there would be no class on Thursday or Friday.

It was the middle of the night on that Wednesday before the holiday. Mimi had been startled awake by the usual stumbling of Mr. Ramirez, creeping in the back door. But this time, he didn't just walk down the hall to his room. This time, he stood in the doorway to the laundry room. Mimi could see him starring at her. She pretended to be asleep but had squinted her eyes just enough so she could see him. The tiny bit of light behind him, that crept in from the broken blind in the kitchen was just enough for Mimi to see him glaring at her as she slept.

Suddenly and without warning, Mr. Ramirez lunged towards Mimi and threw himself on top of her. She had no idea what was happening! She struggled to get him off of her, but he was too heavy. He began groping at her and she started screaming for help! He yelled at her to *'shut up'* and tried to muffle her screams with one hand over her mouth and continued grabbing her with his other hand. Mimi kept trying to scream but he had her mouth closed so tight she couldn't get a sound out. So she bit his hand as hard as she could, just as Mrs. Ramirez grabbed her husband, pulling him off of the terrified young girl.

Mrs. Ramirez began yelling and hitting her husband. He stumble out of the kitchen down the hall to his bedroom. Mimi jumped out of her cot and covered herself with her sheet feeling shame and disbelief at what had just occurred. Mrs. Ramirez became enraged and started yelling at her to get out! She grabbed Mimi's suitcase from under the bed and threw it at her. She screamed, "If you're not out of here in five minutes I'm going to call the police!"

Mimi was in shock and didn't know what to do. She was still trying to catch her breath after what had just happened to her. She didn't know anyone. She couldn't call Dolores because they had no telephone. But she knew she had to get out of there! Sobbing, and in total disbelief as to what had just happened, she began packing what little things she had, and getting dressed. With one hand, she grabbed her school books and with the other hand her suitcase. She ran out the back door as fast as she could. Running down the street in the darkness as tears streamed down her face. She screamed in terror and cried out loud as she ran. She didn't know where she was going but she knew she had to run! Run as fast as she could to get away from there! She ran until she could run no more. Dropping down to her knees, she fell to the ground and continued to sob putting her hands on her face. It took a while before she could stop and breathe. She tried to make sense of what had just happened, but knew she was glad to be out of that house. Wiping the tears off of her face with her blouse, she stood and looked around. She realized she wasn't too far from school. So she walked in that direction. When she got to campus, the only place she thought she could go was to see Mrs. Shear. So, she made her way towards her room and sat outside the door on the floor. Exhausted, she sat pulling her knees close to her face with her arms around her legs. It was there that Mrs. Shear found her when she got to her classroom later that morning.

"Mimi, what are you doing here?" She asked the young girl who sat outside of her classroom with a terrified look on her face.

She helped Mimi to her feet. Mimi threw her arms around her sweet teacher and friend. Mrs. Shear took Mimi inside the class and sat her down on a chair next to her. She then listened in horror as Mimi explained what that man tried to do to her. Fortunately, Mrs. Shear didn't have a class during the first period, and Mimi asked her to please call Mrs. Rodriguez and Dolores to come get her until she could figure out what to do. Trying to console her young talented student, Mrs. Shear agreed to call Mrs. Rodriguez right away. But she re assured Mimi that she'd be welcomed to come home with her if they weren't able to take her in. She locked Mimi in her classroom and went to go call. She only briefly explained that Mimi was sick and needed someone to pick her up. Both she and Dolores came to get her. When they arrived, Mimi and Mrs. Shear explained what had happened. Mrs. Rodriguez and Dolores were drawn to tears hugged Mimi. They told her that she'd be safe with them, and that they would call Sister Barbara Mary. Mrs. Shear asked if she could drop by after school to check on Mimi. And they were grateful to her for helping Dolores's sweet friend.

Mimi was still trembling when she arrived at the Rodriguez house.

"Dolores, please take Mimi to the bathroom and help her get cleaned up."

"Of course. Come I'll show you where everything is. I'll get you some clean clothes."

Dolores helped her friend into her bedroom. Mimi sat on the side of the bed while Dolores looked through her drawers for some things for her. Mimi looked around the room that was now Dolores' home. It had light pink walls and a pretty pink curtains. There were ballerina paintings on the walls.

"You really got lucky with your new family. Mrs. Rodriguez is so nice. You look very happy here. I'm glad for you."

"I wish you had found a nice family too. I can't tell you how sorry I was that your father couldn't take you home. It must really hurt you to have been rejected like that. I can't imagine what you are going through. I'm being adopted! They've really made me part of their family. I'm going to Catholic school. I know it's not cheap, but they treat me like I was their own daughter. I'm very grateful to them for everything they've done for me. But don't worry Mimi, I know Sister Barbara Mary will figure things out you'll see. Those hateful people! I hate what they've put you through. You'll be safe here for now."

Dolores led Mimi to the bathroom so she could bathe. When she got done, Mimi put on the clean clothes her friend had given her and went into the kitchen. Dolores gave her a chair to sit on and began to braid her friend's wet hair.

"Just like old times huh?" She said as she untangled Mimi's beautiful long wavy hair.

"Here, I made you a plate. You must be starving. I want you both to sit and eat everything. Dolores didn't get a chance to eat before we left the house. We have to get strong. Mimi you are too thin. Eat! Drink some milk! It'll make you feel better you'll see."

Mimi was very thankful for the food, but found it hard to eat. She was still much shaken from all that had just happened to her. But the food looked delicious. She hadn't had a real meal that looked this good in a long time. So she forced herself to eat. Mrs. Rodriguez had served them a lovely plate of baked chicken, white rice, black beans and some fried plantains. Even the milk tasted delicious. Every bite she took made her feel better and it tasted great. She'd finished her plate before she knew it.

"You can stay with us as long as it takes to find you a

nice home. We won't let them take you away again unless we're sure you will be treated kindly. There's other homes like ours who love children and will make room for you."

Mrs. Rodriguez hadn't finished the last sentence when there was a knock at the door. She went to see who it was, and came back into the kitchen with Sister Barbara Mary.

"My dear child. I'm so sorry this has happened to you!" She said as she walked towards Mimi and embraced her.

"I wish I had known what animals those people are. It just goes to show you how two faced some parishioners can be. They can be the perfect Catholics at church on Sunday, and at home they are monsters. What are we going to do with you? What are we going to do?"

"She will stay here with us until a decent home turns up." Insisted Mrs. Rodriguez. Sister Barbara Mary took a seat next to Mimi. . She took Mimi's hands between her hands and put her face on top of them. She sobbed and shook her head in disbelief of what had just happened. "You should never have had to endure what happened to you. How will you ever forgive me?"

"I'm tired. Do you think I could lay down somewhere?" Asked Mimi as her eyes filled up with tears again.

"Dolores take Mimi to your room let her take a nap on your bed. You'll be safe there for now. Sleep as long as want. We'll keep an eye out for you. You're safe here."

"Of course said Dolores. Mimi come with me to my room. I'll tuck you in."

Mimi stood up from the table. She looked drawn and exhausted. She followed Dolores into her bedroom and laid on the bed. Dolores took a blanket out her closet and laid it across legs. Mimi rolled over on her side and closed her eyes.

"Sleep now. You need your rest."

Dolores knew her sweet friend was sound asleep in no time. She pulled the blanker over her shoulders and walked out of the room closing the door behind her. She walked back into the kitchen and sat with her Mom and the frail little Nun who was still crying and upset. Mrs. Rodriguez made some Cuban coffee and poured it into the little demitasse cups used to sip it from.

"Here Sister, drink some of this. It'll give you some strength." Mrs. Rodriguez put the little cup in front of Sister Barbara and poured one for herself and Dolores.

"Thank you. I'm going to need it. I feel completely responsible for what's happened. I think we should press charges. When I get back to the camp, I'll call our main parish office and explain what's happened. This just can't just go without some kind of punishment. And I must alert Father Murphy too. He should know. I don't even want to think about what *could have* happened if his wife hadn't intervened as quickly as she did. This is not the way we want these poor children treated when they come to this country."

Mrs. Rodriguez finished sipping her coffee and placed the little cup down on the saucer.

"I only wish *we* could keep her too, but our finances just won't allow it. I know Dolores and Mimi are now like sisters. She'll stay here until you find a safe place for her. I know my husband would insist as well when he hears of this." Mrs. Rodriguez reached for Dolores's hand and squeezed it.

"Thank you Mami. Sister Barbara, did you know I'm being adopted? I'm going to be a real Rodriguez. I love my new family, and I know they love me." Dolores glowed with happiness. "I want her to have what I have. Please find her a real family. She deserves it. She's a really good girl."

"Of course she does. I'm so happy that everything worked out for all of you. I only wish things had turned out different for Mimi with her father. But, we must move forward. I'm going to give her my priority. There aren't any more flights coming in now, and we only have a hand full of kids left in the camps. The Cuban government isn't allowing any more children to leave the island. They stopped all flights last month. It's tragic. So we must do the best we can for the ones that are here."

Sister Barbara reached into her purse and pulled out a white linen hanky. She used it to wipe her face and blow her nose, which made a loud honking sound that took the ladies by surprise! When she stood, she shook hands with Mrs. Rodriguez and hugged Dolores.

"I'll be in touch very soon. Please take good care of her. Dolores, thank you for always looking out for Mimi. God Bless you both."

Mrs. Rodriguez walked the Sister to the door and closed it behind her.

"I'm going to call your father. In the meantime, please go check on her and make sure she's all right."

Dolores crept down the hall and slowly opened the door to her bedroom as not to wake her. Mimi hadn't moved a muscle since she rolled over. Dolores was relieved to see that Mimi was still resting. She certainly needed it after what she'd just gone through.

Chapter 15

It was around four o'clock when Mrs. Rodriguez had another visitor. Mrs. Shear had dropped by as she said she would, to check in on how her sweet student was doing. The girls were in Dolores's bedroom painting their nails and visiting with one another just like old times.

Mrs. Shear was asked to come in the house and took a seat in the living room with Mrs. Rodriguez. She inquired about Mimi and was filled in on the latest. The visit with Sister Barbara Mary assured both of the ladies that Mimi wouldn't come to harm again in the near future. Then Mrs. Shear asked if she might be open to discuss something. She had some news she wanted to share.

"Mrs. Rodriguez, I've grown very fond of Mimi. I don't know if you are aware of the gift this young lady has for the piano? She's an amazing virtuoso. She has the skill and command that doesn't come but once in a life time for a teacher, if ever at all. I've been teaching school for over twenty years and I've had many talented students. But *this young lady,* is far and above any I've ever encountered. Everyone at the school is amazed at what happens when she sits on that bench. She takes control of that keyboard like a trained concert pianist. I've been discussing her with my sister Lisa. She and her husband live in New York and have never had any children. She's a school teacher by profession, but took a job as the head librarian at one of the largest libraries when they moved to the Bronx about ten years ago. Her husband Tom is a banker. They aren't wealthy by any means, but they have a very comfortable life and have a lovely apartment. I was going to have her come to see Mimi play when they visited for Thanksgiving. They're actually arriving this evening. How would you feel about running by them, the possibility of taking Mimi to live with them when they come? That is of course, if everyone is in agreement. They've been considering adopting for the last couple of years. This might be a God sent for everyone?"

"Oh, I don't know. I would have to discuss this with Sister Barbara Mary. And we would have to talk to Mimi. I don't think anyone wants to put her into a bad situation again."

"Of course. I understand. Why don't you discuss it with the Sister and Mimi? I'll talk with my sister and her husband when they get here. They're coming to have Thanksgiving with us. They really are wonderful people. Mimi would be in a stable home, and I know she would never want for anything. Lisa could work with her and we could try to get her into Julliard. I really think she belongs there and has what it takes to get in."

"That would be amazing!" Replied Mrs. Rodriguez as she opened her eyes as wide as they would go. "Dolores has told me that Mimi plays the piano really good, but I've never heard her play. I'll talk to the Sister and to my husband and the girls during dinner tonight. We'll let you know what everyone decides as soon as I have an answer."

"Wonderful. I'll look forward to hearing from you very soon."

After she'd gone, Mrs. Rodriguez walked into the kitchen to use the telephone. She talked to Sister Barbara Mary about what had just been proposed, and she was happy to hear the news. But she was cautious about the situation. Later that evening, she told Mimi what her teacher had suggested. She didn't seem too keen on the idea at first. But agreed to give it some thought.

"I don't know what this Julliard place is?" She said with a puzzled look on her face. Dolores looked at her new Mom also with a questioned look.

Mr. Rodriguez told everyone at the table that he had heard it was a really good school, and that they sent talented students there. Like actors and singers and people that were good at playing instruments. It was a very exclusive school. He told Mimi she would be very lucky to get into a place like that. It would set her career for life.

"I've never thought of playing the piano as a career. I didn't know you could do that. I just thought playing the piano was something to do. I always thought I would go to school to become a teacher, or a doctor or something."

"Oh yes!" Exclaimed Mr. Rodriguez. "You can get a degree there."

"Well, I guess it's easier than having to read all those books you have to read to become a doctor!" She said and began to laugh. And so did everyone else at the table. Dolores was happy to see her friend relax and enjoy her evening with a family that she felt comfortable with. She was glad to see her friend smile. Something she didn't get to see often when they first met.

In the morning, the girls went into the kitchen to get breakfast and saw Mrs. Rodriguez putting a big turkey into the oven. Dolores's new little sister was sitting at the table eating Kellogg's cornflakes. She was still in her pajamas, and had terrible bad hair. Dolores walked over to the table and took a seat next to her. She reached over and gave the young girl a kiss. Mimi sat next to her and they watched Mrs. Rodriguez close the oven door and set a timer.

"I'm going to have to braid that mop you have on your

head this morning." Said Dolores to Carla as she ran her fingers through her nappy hair.

"Dolores, you should be a hairdresser when you grow up." Said Mimi to her friend. "You're always braiding hair."

"Maybe I will be. I like fixing hair. So what is this Thanksgiving everyone is talking about. We don't have this in Cuba."

Mrs. Rodriguez washed her hands and put a bowl in front of the girls, then began to pour them some cereal and milk.

"Well, it's an American holiday. It's when the Pilgrims came to America and ate with the Indians."

"Oh Mami!" Laughed Carla. "It's more than that. I'll read my history book to you later. You both have to learn about the holidays here. There's more celebrating here than in Cuba. There we only had Christmas and Carnival. Here, they celebrate lots of things. But today, we eat turkey just like the Pilgrims, and pie. Mami you didn't forget the pie did you?"

"Your Tia is bringing the pie. If she forgets, you can be mad at her. Mimi, you'll get to meet the rest of the family later. Everyone is coming. Its Dolores's first Thanksgiving. And yours too of course."

Dolores whispered to Carla, "What are Pilgrims and...

what kind of pie?"

"Don't worry. Pie is pie." Laughed Mrs. Rodriguez. "And this isn't going to be a real *traditional* dinner like the Americans have. It's sort of is, but with a Cuban flare. No mash potatoes. We make Congri! You know what that is don't you Mimi? Did your family make it? You know, white rice smothered with black beans?"

"Ay! I haven't had good Cuban food since I got here to America. In fact, here in your home is the first time I've really gotten to eat *real* Cuban food. I'm so happy! At the camp they fed us American food. Half the time I'd never even heard of what it was. But I did eat the mashed potatoes. They were good."

Dolores rolled her eyes back into her head. "Mashed potatoes was about the only thing that tasted good in that place. Everything else was weird. Like, what is *macaroni and cheese*? We never ate that in Cuba."

"Well, said Mrs. Rodriguez, "You'll eat well here in my house. I don't know how to cook American food. And you need to gain some weight. You're nothing but skin and bones."

Later that afternoon, their family began to arrive. They all brought plates of food to share. Someone brought 'Yuka', someone else brought some delicious fresh baked bread. And fried plantains. Mrs. Rodriguez finished the turkey and Mr. Rodriguez carved it. The family came together around the table and gave thanks for all of the food. They gave thanks for all the blessings they had been given in their new country. And, they gave thanks for the new member of the family: Dolores…..And her new friend.

Mimi was never so grateful for anything in her life. She sat and ate among people she could relate to. Everyone laughed, made jokes, and spoke Spanish- loud! They talked about everything. From their jobs, to politics. To that she listened intently. Not realizing until this moment how naïve she had been in her little world back home. How sheltered she had been. Not knowing anything that had been happening in her country. It wasn't until she arrived in the U.S. that she had begun to hear bits and pieces of how life had changed in her old world. She sat there watching, and wondered about *her* family back home. There hadn't been any word from anyone. She had sent a couple of letters, but the Castro regime was filtering all of the mail leaving the island. And had gone as far as to stop the flow of correspondence. So she had no news from anyone. But at this moment, the loneliness she had felt wasn't as strong. These were good hard working and caring people, who had given up everything they once had in order to live a life of Freedom and Democracy. This is what they wanted for their children. Like Dolores's grandmother who had made the great sacrifice to send away the only relative she had left, in order for her to find a better life than what she would have had if she had stayed. *Now* she got it. She knew why she had been put on that plane and what she was doing here in this country. And, she knew she had to honor them for their sacrifice. She still wasn't going to give up the hope that they would someday be reunited, but knew she had to do something great with her life. That was a defining moment in her life. Her first Thanksgiving. And so with a silent prayer of her own, she gave thanks. And she made the decision that she would stop feeling sorry for herself. From that day forward, she was going to own her life. She was going to be someone special. Looking around the room, she smiled and asked, "Hey! Where's the pie?"

Chapter 16

Sister Barbara Mary had a meeting with Mrs. Shear and the Boxwells at her office on Friday after the holiday. They all met to discuss Mimi's situation and to get to know one another. She asked hard questions of the couple and watched them very carefully as they answered. She observed their body language, and their interaction with one another. Tom seemed like a well-educated man who still held hands with his wife as they entered her office. He was soft spoken and jolly. He was of average size and weight with soft brown eyes and hair with graying temples. Lisa was an attractive woman also of average weight and height. She had soft hazel eyes and wavy dark blonde hair which she kept shoulder length. Both very well dressed and groomed. She had a nice smile and looked very much like her Sister Mrs. Shear.

Sister Barbara Mary had asked the Rodriguez's and Dolores to bring Mimi to the camp at around three o'clock for that meeting. Mimi was to play the piano for everyone when she arrived. Once everyone had introduced themselves, they took seats around a table in Sister Barbara's office, and it was Mimi's turn to ask questions of the couple. She asked where they lived and what they did. Both the Boxwells spoke enough Spanish to get by. By now, Mimi's English had improved and was more fluent from speaking in class and at school. The Rodriguez's sat in the back of the room and watched the interaction. Mrs. Rodriguez was being very apprehensive and wanted to make sure Mimi wouldn't be placed in harm's way again.

Mimi asked why they would want to become Foster Parents to a person of her age after having been married and childless for so long. She asked why not wait for a baby? Mr. Boxwell, in a joking manner said, "You don't require burping do you?"

Everyone laughed. Even Sister Barbara Mary laughed. "Well shall we make our way into the chapel?" She asked. Everyone followed her inside and took a seat on one of the pews. Mimi walked over to the white piano she hadn't touched in what seemed like ages. She sat on the bench and lifted the cover. The room became silent and they watched Mimi close her eyes and take a deep breath. Now placing her hands on the ivory, she began to play Beethoven's Moonlight Sonata.

As she played, the music seemed to magically fill the small room. Everyone's mouths dropped open. Sister Barbara Mary watched the Boxwells reaction. Mrs. Shear leaned forward and listened intently as her student glided her hands from one end of the key board to the other. She closed her eyes and used her index finger in a motion as if she were directing her. Her heard rocked slowly from side to side as she felt the music through her body. Both couples were moved to tears.

When she finished, everyone applauded. Mrs. Boxwell stood and made her way to Mimi. She put her arms around her and was so overcome with emotion that she was unable to speak. The music had obviously touched her deeply.

. Everyone thanked her for playing for them and Mrs. Shear told the Rodriguez's she would call them very soon. They left with Mimi and Dolores, but before they parted, Mr. Boxwell hugged Mimi and said, "We sure hope to see you again very soon Mimi."

Sister Barbara Mary, Mrs. Shear and the Boxwells returned to the office. They were so taken by the music, Mrs. Boxwell was still tearing up.

"So, where do we go from here?" Asked Sister Barbara.

Mrs. Boxwell began the conversation by saying, "She's amazing." She looked at her sister and said. "You were right. This young lady belongs at Julliard. We just can't let her disappear into the world without nurturing this gift.

And she's absolutely lovely! You can tell she's been well brought up in a good home. I'm sure Tom would agree it would be a blessing to us if we were allowed to have her in our lives."

"Oh, it goes without saying. She would be a light in our home. And we would give her a family. There's already a piano in our apartment. And Lisa can help tutor her so she could pass the GED while we do all of the applications to get her to Julliard.

"Well…" Said the relieved Nun, "I'll have to do some sort of background investigation and will need some references. And the ultimate decision will have to be Mimi's."

Mrs. Shear beamed "I'm delighted! I so wanted to help this young lady from the moment she walked into my classroom. Just think, I'll get to become her auntie!"

Sister Barbara added. "Mr. and Mrs. Boxwell, thank you for considering this. God has his plan. Hopefully my investigation will be the answer we're *all* looking for, and in the best interest of the child of courses. I'll be in touch with you as soon as I'm satisfied with everything."

Mr. Boxwell reached into his shirt pocket. "Sister, here is my business card for the bank. I've been there for over ten years. We're leaving for New York tomorrow but you can reach me at that number any time. Let me know what else we can provide to you so you can be comfortable in your decision."

"Thank you all for coming and thank you for being such lovely people. By the way, her father, is willing to sign adoption papers if you should get to that point in the future, and would like to make it official. But I guess we'll cross that bridge if we get there. I'll be in touch."

For the next week, Sister Barbara was on the telephone getting as much information as she could on the couple. From employment references to personal ones. Even from the church they attended. When she was satisfied she called Mrs. Shear at her home and asked her to meet with her at the Rodriguez house the following day. She made arrangements with Mr. and Mrs. Rodriguez to come to their house after supper to meet with Mrs. Shear and Mimi. When they arrived, everyone went into the kitchen and sat around the table. Dolores took a seat next to her friend.

"Well," smiled Sister Barbara Mary "I must say these are the nicest people I've ever investigated. They seem to be upstanding citizens, good members of the church hard-working people. The neighbors all seem to think that they are wonderful. Their employers had nothing but great things to say about them. I just couldn't find anything wrong with them, and they seem to be truly sincere about taking Mimi in. So with that in mind, Mimi how would you feel about going to live in New York with Mr. and Mrs. Boxwell?"

"Mimi my sister and brother-in-law are really wonderful people and they're so looking forward to your coming to live with them. They will do everything they can to make you happy and see that you get a good education. I don't think it's a decision that you ever regret making. They will give you a good home and see to your every need. I can drive you up there myself. I have vacation time coming in two weeks and we can make an adventure of it. It's up to you of course. And I can bring you back if you're not comfortable when I leave."

Mrs. Rodriguez looked at Mimi. She had a half smile on her face but still had some hesitation in her eyes. "Mimi if you don't like it there you're always welcome to come back and stay with us until we find just the right place. Don't feel that you can't ever come back here. You're like a sister to Dolores, and Carla adores you. We're family to you now as well. So don't ever think that you're not welcome back. Why not give it a try? If you don't think it's the right fit we'll welcome you back."

Sister Barbara Mary looked at everyone in the room and said.

"Well Mimi what do you think? Shall we give this a

try? It sounds like you just may have found your new family. And even after Mrs. Shear leaves, you're welcome to call me at any time and I will be up there to get you lickety-split! We all have your best interest in mind and getting a good education is very important to us. You have such an amazing gift. If you can get into Julliard your career will be all but set. And we think that with the talent that you have, you're destined to become a very famous pianist."

Mimi took a deep breath and looked around the room at everyone seated at the table. She smiled and nodded her head and said.

"Yes I'll go. I hope my new family is just as wonderful as Dolores's family. If I get just half as lucky as she has I'll be ever so thankful. I know my family wanted what's best for me in America and that's why they sent me to live here. I know that they trusted that God would find a way for me. So I have to trust as well. If I don't try I might regret not taking this opportunity." Mimi looked at Mrs. Shear and asked. "When can we leave?"

Mrs. Shear clapped her hands over her mouth and said.

"Oh that's wonderful! They're going to be very happy Mimi! And you will too. Just wait and see. I'll call them just as soon as I get home."

As Mrs. Rodriguez stood up and said. "Well this calls

for a celebration. I have some left over apple pie and ice cream why don't I get us all a plate?"

Dolores gave her friend Mimi a big hug.

"I'm going to miss you so much Mimi. You have to write me letters every day and tell me all about New York. Maybe someday I'll get to come and visit. Mami, do you think I can go to visit Mimi in New York someday?"

"Of course! We'll all go. I've always wanted to visit New York. We'll have to make it a family vacation." Mr. Rodriguez began eating his ice cream and cake while looking at Mimi and said.

"Sounds like a good idea. We'll all come to see you Mimi and you can show us your new city."

"Well it's settled then." said Sister Barbara Mary. "New York with the Boxwells it is. I'm very please for you Mimi. I think you've been the toughest one of my kids to place. You're very special. I'm not happy that we can't get any more children out of the island and away from Castro. There are still thousands waiting to come. But I'm certainly pleased that I've been entrusted with the future of so many wonderful children. I pray every day for every one of them. But you Mimi, will always get an extra special prayer."

Chapter 17

On Saturday December 22, on the eve of the winter solstice, Mimi and Mrs. Shear arrived at her new home in Queens New York. Mimi had been in awe while driving into the city. She'd never seen buildings so tall in her life. Nor had she been on bridges so long. It was as if she had just arrived on a new planet. Everything was so different. Even from Miami.

The sky was blistery and cold....so cold! Mimi had never experienced snow! Getting out of the car, Mrs. Shear had given Mimi one of her coats to use. It fit too big, but it was keeping her warm. Snow was on the ground and they expected more within the next twenty four hours. It was to be her first White Christmas. Her eyes teared from the cold, and her nose was running.

"Well Mimi, this is going to be your new home." She said as she pointed up to the top of a six story walk up. This too seemed high for someone who had never been above a second story in a home or in a building. Mr. Boxwell had been looking out for them from the front window and came out the front door of the building to greet them with a smile and big hugs for both.

"Welcome! Welcome Mimi. We're so happy that you're here. Let me take the suitcases upstairs. Lisa is waiting with some hot chocolate upstairs." That sounded so good to Mimi right now. She was chilled to the bone.

When the entered the building, Mimi took a look around. There was a wall with mailboxes numbered for each apartment. The tile on the floor was a bit muddy from people's dirty feet due to the weather, but you could tell it was beautifully maintained black and white checkered. Mr. Boxwell let the way up the seemingly endless set stairs. When they finally arrived at the sixth floor, they had reached the top. There were two apartments. One on each side of the landing.

"This way." He pointed to the door on the right. He set the suitcases down and opened the door.

"Lisa, they're here!" He hollered with excitement in his voice. Mrs. Boxwell walked out of the kitchen door just as they were stepping inside. She was carrying a serving tray and four mugs. Steam was coming out of all of them and the smell was wonderful. She set them down on the coffee table and approached Mimi.

"Welcome!" She said while giving her a big hug. "We're so glad you're here. I hope you like your room." She walked over and gave her sister a kiss and thanked her for taking the three day drive up from Miami. "Looks like you ladies made some pretty good time traveling considering the weather is like it is. Please sit, have some cocoa."

Cocoa, thought Mimi? Cocoa was coconut in Spanish. Could there be hot *coconut* in the cups she wondered? She slipped off her coat and Mr. Boxwell took it to the coat closet to hang up. She and Mrs. Shear took a seat on the lovely sofa. Mimi was very pleased at what she saw. The room reminded her of her Tia and Tio's house in Havana. It had ceiling to floor windows with beautiful window coverings. The furniture was all newer and the paintings on the walls were of lovely flower arrangements. There was an upright piano against one wall, and two arm chairs facing the sofa. Everyone took a seat. Mrs. Boxwell handed Mimi a mug and asked her to drink. It smelled delicious, and Mimi blew into the cup to cool it just a bit before tasting it.

"What are those white things on top?" She asked

"Why, those are marshmallows. You've never had them?"

"No, but they look good." With that, she took her first sip and a smile came over her face.

"This is hot chocolate!" She exclaimed. "I thought you said it was cocoa. To me that means cocoanut."

Mrs. Shear and the Boxwells laughed and that caught

Mimi by surprise.

"Chocolate is made from cocoa beans. So sometimes we refer to it as 'cocoa'. But you are right. It is *hot chocolate*. There will be lots for you to learn here in your new country. But don't worry. We're here to help you learn about everything. Don't worry if you don't understand something. Just ask."

They went about making conversation Mimi noticed a Christmas tree in one of the corners of the living room. She asked what it was doing there? Mr. Boxwell explained that they had purchased the tree for the Christmas holiday but had waited decorated it so that she could help. Mimi explained that in Cuba, this Christmas is celebrated on January 6 when the three Wise men visited baby Jesus. She also explained that on the eve of December 24 they celebrated what was called *Noche Buena*-Christmas Eve. This was the main celebration for churchgoing as it is the eve prior to Christ's birth. Most everyone attended church celebrated the midnight mass and night services. But she seemed excited about decorating the Christmas tree. At home Abuela always decorate the tree when no one was home and she never really got to help with the decorating. She asked when they could decorate the tree and was told they could do it that evening after dinner if she wanted to. This seemed to please her.

"Would you like to see your bedroom?" Asked Mrs. Boxwell.

"Yes thank you."

Mrs. Boxwell led Mimi down the hall followed by Mrs. Shear. When they entered, Mimi stood for a moment and looking at what was to be her new room.

"I hope you like it."

"I don't know what to say!" Mimi found it hard to find the words. "It's so beautiful. I don't know how to thank you."

"Oh, it was no trouble. We want you to feel right at home here. *This* is home now. This is your own space. If there is anything you think you might need we want you to tell us."

The room was painted white. Behind the bed and on the corresponding wall, hung white wall paper decorated with an Ivy pattern. There were lace curtains that criss crossed in front of the windows. The bed was covered with a white ruffled lace bedspread and was adorned with green satin throw pillows. There was a desk and a makeup table. On the walls hung framed photographs of Cuba.

"Do you like the photographs? Tom and I went to Cuba on our honeymoon. These are some of the pictures he took. We thought they might make you feel less home sick. I especially like the ones that have the Royal Palms in them."

Mimi didn't have words. Her eyes welled up with tears that began to stream down her cold face. She walked over to Mrs. Boxwell and put her arms around her then began to cry. She missed her family and her home. And she missed her friend Antonio. She remembered the two of them sitting in the tree house looking at Royal Palms for as far as the eye could see. That picture reminded her of this and it overwhelmed her. She wondered where everyone at home was, and if they missed her too.

Mrs. Shear walked over to the both of them and they all hugged. "There there…." She said as she got teary herself. "You're in a safe place now. We're your family."

Mimi was finally able to utter, "thank you." But somehow that didn't seem enough.

Mrs. Boxwell wanted to unpack Mimi's suitcase so she could get all settled in. When they opened it, they noticed there wasn't much to unpack. She'd come with so little, and most of it was now so worn she'd have to have some new clothes. "We're going to have to go shopping! You need some new clothes. Especially here in New York. You don't have a single think in here to keep you warm."

Mimi reached into her suitcase. She had brought with her a Cuban cook book that Mrs. Rodriguez had purchased for Mrs. Boxwell and gave it to her. She laughed and promised she would learn to cook Cuban food for her. Then, she pulled out the photograph she had brought from her Tia's house. The one of her, and her Mom playing the piano when she was a little girl. She placed it on the night stand next to her bed.

"Is that your Mama?"

"Yes, she used to put me on her lap when she played piano when I was little. I would watch her and sometimes she'd put my hands on hers while she played. She played so pretty. I wanted to play just like her. So when she died, my Abuela had teachers come to the plantation to give me lessons. Sometimes, my Papi would sit and watch us and she would sing to him."

Mrs. Boxwell smiled at Mimi and told her she had a surprise for her. She reached under the bed and brought out a box wrapped in lovely Santa Claus paper and tied with a pretty red ribbon.

"We were going to give this to you later this week, but I see now this is something you're going to need right away. Go ahead, open it!"

The surprise made Mimi smile bigger than she'd smiled in ages. She carefully untied the ribbon and removed the paper. When she finally got through it all of the tissue paper, she pulled out a pair of red flannel pajamas, a red flannel robe and a pair of furry slipper. She felt the soft material and rubbed it over her cheek. She'd never worn flannel before. She held everything up to her to see how it would look.

"These are beautiful! I think they'll keep me very warm. Thank you Mrs. Boxwell."

"Now, we're going to have to change that. Don't you think you might like to call us something a little less formal? How about just Lisa and Tom? You're family now. Mr. and Mrs. is just too old fashioned. How would you feel about that?"

"That would be just fine. Lisa. I like your name."

After dinner, they all helped decorate the tree. The Boxwells and Mrs. Shear loved watching Mimi smile. Mimi played Silent Night on the Piano. She seemed really happy and was having a good time. For a moment, she forgot everything that she had gone through.

Later that evening, Mimi got ready for bed. She put on her new pajamas and robe. She came out to model them for everyone and they all said their good nights. She crawled into her nice new bed in her beautiful new room. It was comfortable and she felt warm and safe. She felt at peace for the first time since she'd left her home.

Saying a prayer of thanks and praying for her family as she always did, she wished there had been some word from her family back home. She'd sent several letters, but they'd always gone unanswered. All she could do was to have faith that someday, she would get some word from them. Then she slept.

Chapter 18

Following one of the coldest winters on record with temperatures hitting an all-time low of minus four degrees, the Boxwells went about trying to immerse Mimi into what was now to become her new culture. Mrs. Boxwell had taken her to 'Mays' department store and purchased her much needed new clothes, and a beautiful warm coat that fit. They would take her to the movies on Saturday night and always walked to attend Sunday Mass. Sometimes after church, if the weather permitted, they would go to breakfast. Mimi had discovered pancakes and loved to pour maple syrup all over the top. She'd found her new family at last, and had become very fond of this couple who had taken her in and shown her so much love and affection. She especially loved the humor in their lives and how happy they were together. Mimi imagined her parents would have been the same way had her mother lived. She knew how very much *they* had loved each other.

The three of them visited the board of education and explained Mimi's exceptional circumstance. The Boxwells thought it best that she be tutored at home, so she could focus on her music. Fortunately, Mrs. Boxwells teaching degree and her connections at the Library played in their favor, and were granted the permission to do so. Mrs. Boxwell was to tutor her so she would be able to pass the GED exam which would be necessary for acceptance to Julliard. Every day, she and Mimi would take the subway train to the Public Library on forty second and fifth where she worked. There, she was able to keep an eye on Mimi while she did her studies. She had to bring Mimi up to speed on World and American History. The mathematics studies were Mr. Boxwells part. He'd always been in finance, and his knowledge in that department benefited Mimi. Fortunately for them, she was a quick study.

They also interviewed piano teachers. During their tour and initial visit to the Manhattan School of Music, they'd gotten a list of possibilities, as well as the requirements for admission to Julliard. The conservatory was about to move to a new location on Claremont Avenue, and Mimi would attend classes there if she were to be selected.

After interviewing several teachers, they settled on a woman who had been a concert pianist when she was young. Ariana Bierman. Unfortunately, arthritis had settled into her hands and became unable to continue performing. She had at one time, been on the faculty at Julliard and was now semi-retired. Miss Bierman and Mimi hit it off right away.

Miss. Bierman sat with perfect posture on the edge of the sofa. She had crazy frizzy salt and pepper hair that trailed down to the middle of her back in a very bohemian style. She was very thin and had knots on her fingers from the arthritis. She discussed her resume in quite detail with the Boxwells and Mimi. She was a graduate of the Moscow Music Conservatory and had been the winner of countless competitions. She'd performed with many of the world's orchestras and conductors. She said she'd never married, but bragged about having many famous conductors and musicians as lovers. Something the Boxwells thought was a bit *too much* information. She was quite the quirky character, but they all liked her right away.

Before accepting the proposed position, she insisted Mimi sit with her at the piano and play. They both sat on the bench and Miss. Bierman pulled some sheet music out of her rather large purse. She watched her student intently. Periodically, she would run her hand down Mimi's back and say, "Posture my dear-posture." Mimi would sit up and continue to play. Miss. Bierman made comments now and then, but seemed to be impressed.

This went on for an hour. Mr. and Mrs. Boxwell both sat wringing their fingers. They waited to see what the teacher would say. Finally, after Mimi had gone through all of the music, Miss. Bierman turned back around and looked at them.

"Well, she does show promise. I think I can work with her. She's a bit rusty, but we'll get her up to speed before the audition. She's going to have to work very hard you know? I've served on the admission 'Jury' at the conservatory and I know what they are looking for. It's possible with constant work she may make it. I'll be her Monday, Wednesday and Friday. I will arrive promptly at twelve thirty and we will study until four. Before and after my arrival, I expect she will be practicing the music I assign her. That goes for the other two days of the week. There is to be at least five hours a day of practice or I assure you she won't make it. Practice, practice, practice! Are you willing to do that?" She asked Mimi.

"Of course. I want this to be my profession, and I want to make my family proud."

"Well then, enough said. You will practice the music I've given you, and I will see you tomorrow promptly at twelve thirty."

Miss Bierman stood and walked quickly towards the door. Mr. Boxwell ran to open it for her.

"Thank you Miss. Bierman. I know Mimi won't let you down. We can't tell you how happy we are that you'll be working with her."

After Miss Bierman left, Mrs. Boxwell clapped and congratulated Mimi. "You're going to be famous someday. I just know it! Wasn't she funny though?" They all agreed she was a bit strange but liked her very much.

And so that following Monday, there was a knock at the door at exactly twelve thirty. Mimi ran to let Miss. Bierman in. They immediately got to work. Miss. Bierman reached into her big purse and pulled out a small long thin black case, and removed a conductor's baton from inside. She asked Mimi to play for her the music she had left for her, and stood behind her watching her every move. As her new student easily moved her hands on the keyboard, she paced back and forth waving the baton to the music as if she was conducting her, occasionally making comments about her tempo or reminding her about her posture.

"You must sit up straight so you can *breathe* the notes from your soul into your fingers. Breathe Mimi, breathe."

For the next few months, Mimi withstood the grueling schedule. Practice with Miss. Bierman three days a week, library with Mrs. Boxwell and math instruction with Mr.

Boxwell. Leaving the weekend for more practice and very little else. But the Boxwells would try to make sure she was learning more than just piano and school work. On weekends, they visited the Empire State Building and the Statue of Liberty. They'd take her to see plays like Oliver on Broadway, and concerts by the New York Philharmonic to see Leonard Bernstein conduct. She loved his performance of the music for West Side Story, and told the Boxwells she would someday be on the stage with that orchestra. Immersing her in music and theater every chance they could. They felt this was vital to her future. And she appreciated it very much. She'd never attended any professional performances in Cuba and was more sure than ever that this was the life she wanted. To perform on stage for a live audience. And her dream since she was little, was to perform at Carnegie Hall. She felt she owed it to her Abuela, who had inspired her to play music by telling her stories about attending concerts there. That, was her dream.

In June, she was ready to take the test for the G.E.D. And on that day, Mr. Boxwell took the day off from work so that he could go with her and Mrs. Boxwell. They were more nervous than she was. Together they walked into the New York Department of Education office, and looked for the room where she was to take the exam. The Boxwells hugged Mimi at the door and told her they would be waiting for her outside while she completed the two hour exam. When the doors closed, Mimi listened to the Proctor give the instructions. When she was told to do so, she and the twelve other people in the room turned over the papers on the desks and began the test. Mimi glanced at the clock on the wall, then started to read. She'd been practicing her reading in English with Mrs. Boxwell and felt confident in her understanding of the exam questions. After only an hour and forty minutes, she put her pencil down and turned her paper back over. The Proctor saw that she was done and signaled her to bring it up to her desk. After a quick glance to make sure all of the questions had been answered, she told Mimi she was dismissed and was told that she would receive a letter in the mail informing her of her results.

Mr. and Mrs. Boxwell took Mimi out to lunch to celebrate and when they got back to the apartment, Mrs. Boxwell asked Mimi to call Dolores and catch up with her. She'd been so busy with studies and piano, she really hadn't had time to call or write. Mimi was excited to do so. Mrs. Boxwell could hear Mimi giggling and talking is Spanish to her friend. It made her smile to know how well Mimi was doing and how quickly she was adapting to her new country. The next hurdle was the audition for Julliard that was to be in the next month, on July 15. The day after Mimi's sixteenth birthday. But she was sure she was ready. Her command of the piano was amazing, and under the instruction of Miss. Bierman, she had become even better.

Two weeks later, Mimi had gone downstairs to get the mail. She always hoped that somehow, her family had been notified of where she was living and that there would be a letter from home. And as always, there was nothing. But, she was surprised to find that there was a letter addressed to her. When Mimi looked at the return address on left corner she saw that it was from the New York Department of Education. She ran up the stairs and handed it to Mrs. Boxwell. She was out of breath. "Look I think this is the letter lets open it, I can't wait to see if I passed!"

"Of course you passed she said as she handed the letter back to Mimi and told her to open it."

"Here you open it it's addressed to you. Quickly open it!"

"My hands are shaking I can't get it opened."

She tore open the envelope she felt a knot in her stomach. When she pulled out the neatly folded paper that was inside, she began to read the letter out loud.

"Dear Mr. Bennis, this letter is to inform you that you

have passed the New York Department of Education G.E.D. exam. Enclosed is your certificate of completion. Congratulations. We wish you the best and encourage you to continue further education."

"I passed I passed! I'm so happy I passed thank you for helping me! I couldn't have done it without you and Tom. I can't wait to tell him when he gets home."

"Well this calls for a special celebration. I'm going to cook you a Cuban dinner tonight. I've been reading the recipes the book that Mrs. Rodriguez sent me and I think I have everything that I need. You can help me if you'd like."

"Oh I'd really like that but I'm afraid I'm not much of a cook. I think it's best if I just sit at the piano and practice so that Miss Bierman doesn't fuss at me when she gets here. You know how she can tell if I haven't been putting hundred percent into my practices. What are you going to make?"

"I thought I would take a stab at Arroz con Pollo. That's chicken with rice, no?"

"Yes it's one of my favorites. And will you fry up some bananas too?"

"I'm going to do my best. I was able to find some plantains at the outdoor market. We'll have lots to celebrate when Tom gets home. You go on and practice.

Leave the cooking to me. I'm going to surprise you!"

Mimi thanked Mrs. Boxwell and ran to the piano to begin her practice. Her happy mood reflected in her music. She played until Mr. Boxwell arrived from work. Dinner turned out to be pretty good for her first attempt at Cuban food. It wasn't quite like back home, but it was pretty close and Mimi appreciated her attempt. The bananas were a little overcooked by Mimi was so happy just to have them that she never mentioned a word. She couldn't believe how lucky she had been ending up with these two lovely people that cared so deeply for her. And she knew she must take on her next hurdle full on. Her education at Julliard would put her one step closer to her dream of becoming a concert pianist.

During dinner Mr. Boxwell would occasionally talk to Mimi what he had read in the paper or what he had heard was happening in Cuba. But she knew that there was nothing she could do about solving the problems of the world. All she could do was to move forward with her life and become someone her family would be proud of, but still hoping they could re unite someday.

Chapter 19

Mimi awoke on July 14, 1963 in the place now called home. Exactly one year ago, she'd left her home and her family. So much had happened in just 12 months. Her entire life had now changed. She lived in a new country where so much was different than what she was accustomed to. From the language to the weather, to the food to the people that surrounded her. Everything was different. She was grateful for what she'd been given because she knew that not everyone that had come under the same circumstances of the Peter Pan flights, had been as lucky as she had been. Dolores had told her stories that she'd heard at school or that her new parents had heard about. The good and the bad that happened to many of the children that had come on those flights. Many had found nice Foster homes, or were being adopted by families her in the United States. But others were being treated as second-class citizens or had left the homes they had been placed in and were living homeless on the streets of different cities and states. But a year had come and gone and not a single letter from home. Not one of her letters had been answered. She was happy and sad at the same time.

At breakfast that morning, Mr. and Mrs. Boxwell gave her a gold charm bracelet with a piano charm as a gift for her 16th birthday. They told her that they knew that in Cuba most young ladies are given a *Quincenllera* celebration to celebrate a coming of age at age fifteen. But in America, young ladies celebrated the same but at age sixteen. And today she would have a chance to celebrate, but a year later. They also wanted to celebrate the anniversary of her arrival in America and how fortunate they were that she had come to be part of their family.

That evening they were going to the ballet. They wanted to take Mimi's mind off of everything. Her audition for the Julliard School was to be the next day. They knew her mind was going to be on overload, thinking about her family back home, and trying not to stress about the exam the next day. Mrs. Boxwell brought out a box from her bedroom and gave it to Mimi. It was beautifully wrapped and there was a card that wished her a very Happy Birthday. The gift was from Mrs. Shear. Mimi opened it carefully and inside she found a beautiful pastel pink tulle gown to wear that evening to the ballet. It was the most beautiful dress she had ever seen! If she could have picked it out herself, she couldn't have done a better job. She asked Mrs. Boxwell if she could call her to thank her. Mrs. Boxwell also gave her a card that had come in the mail from Sister Barbara Mary wishing her a very Happy Birthday and encouraging her to do her best at her audition.

That evening during the performance, Mimi's mind got lost in what was happening on stage, and in the music. She watched the conductor intently. Her fingers moving to the music while in her mind she played along on the piano with the orchestra.

In the morning Mrs. Boxwell made sure that Mimi had a large breakfast. She fixed her pancakes since that was her favorite. Then they all took the train to the Conservatory.

Mimi's audition was set for 11 o'clock. They had been instructed to arrive one hour early and were assigned a warm-up room. The air conditioned place was a welcomed relief as the ride in had been a hot one. New York was cooking that time of the year. The place was crawling with young people. All hopefuls of passing their auditions in being given the opportunity to attend the conservatory. Mimi was taken to a practice room and began to warm up on the piano, while Mr. and Mrs. Boxwell sat quietly in a corner. At about 10:50 a woman entered the room and asked Mimi to follow her. The

Boxwells stood and gave Mimi hugs and wished her good luck. Mimi didn't feel nervous and was confident in her music selection. She was led down several halls and into the concert auditorium where she was escorted onto the stage. There in the middle sat a beautiful Bosendorfer Grand Piano. As she walked towards it, she could hear her footsteps echoing in the large stage. Mimi had never played on a piano as opulent as this one. She walked to the center of the stage and turned to face the Selection Jury. She took a moment to look around at all the seats and looked up at the balcony. The place was empty except for the professors of the Jury. She was asked to introduce herself and give them a brief description of why she wanted to attend Julliard. Mimi gave them a quick synopsis of the last year of her life. She told them of her flight from Cuba and explained that she was one of the Peter Pan children. She told them how important it was for her to honor her family, and that her admission to Julliard was crucial in accomplishing her dream of becoming a concert pianist.

They thanked her and asked her to begin when she was ready. Mimi walked over to the piano, took a seat and adjusted her bench. Then she ran her fingers across the keys almost as if she was introducing herself to them. She took a deep breath, closed her eyes and sat straight on the bench. She could almost hear Miss. Bierman reminding her of her posture. Then she began. She had selected Chopin's Concerto in e minor. She played for about fifteen minutes as this was the time frame she'd been given. She had practiced timing herself at home and knew about where to end. As she played she felt herself getting caught up in the music. It was her first time on a big stage but she felt very much at home there. It was as if she was she was there alone in the large room. Just her and the piano. There were no nerves and no doubt that she was up for the task. She'd rehearsed until the music was fluid from her fingertips to the keys. The sound the music made as she played echoed in the large chamber. It was a sound like none she had ever heard before. Almost as if she was being introduced to her playing for the first time. Of course she'd heard pianos playing in the concert halls at the performances she had attended with the Boxwells. But this time, she was hearing it from the stage side, and not the audience side. She liked what she heard. An adrenalin rush came over her that she'd never experienced before.

When she was finished, she put her hands on her lap and exhaled. Thankful that it was over, but at the same time, sad that she had to stop playing on the beautiful piano. She stood and thanked the jury. As she left the stage she noticed many of them making notes and whispering to one another. She was escorted back to the lobby where she met up with the Boxwells. Now all they could do was wait until they were notified. Again, another letter. Patience and time was all they had to look forward to. And so they would have to wait. But she was confident that she'd done her best and knew that she had not felt alone on that stage. Mr. Boxwell had taken them down the street to a Jewish Deli for Pastrami sandwiches. When they were waiting for their food, she told the Boxwells that she had felt her mother's presence while she was up on stage. Almost as if she'd been there giving her strength and confidence when she played. Mrs. Boxwell told Mimi not to discount her feelings. She believed that the Angel Spirits of the people that loved us the most always come stand by our side when we need them, and she told her not to be afraid.

Although there was no more schoolwork that needed to be done during the rest of this summer, the piano practice had to continue. There was no 'plan B'. If she didn't' get in, they hadn't really discussed another option.

Miss. Bierman had skipped class with Mimi on the day of the audition, but had made plans to come on Tuesday instead, and pick up with their regular routine on Wednesday. She was hopeful that things would turn out as they all hoped they would. So the practice continued, and they waited. Until the following Monday. When the letter arrived congratulating- *Miss. Maribel Bennis of her acceptance to the Julliard School of Music to peruse her education towards her Bachelor of Music Degree.* Life was about to change for Mimi once again. She'd be one of the youngest students at the school.

"I had no doubt you'd make it young lady. Bravo!" Said Miss Bierman as she bowed in front of her student. "Now go and give'm hell!"

And in September of that year, she walked through the doors of the Julliard School of Music, fresh and excited to get started. There were a large number of students in the lobby. She waited there until they called the new music students into one of the large classrooms to begin a brief introduction of their program and what to expect from the first week. Each student was then placed into different sections depending on their instruments. Then, they were each assigned a professor with whom they would be studying under.

Mimi was assigned to Professor Barry Hamilton. A portly man in his early sixties. He was bald on top and had a ring of overgrown white hair circling the circumference of his head. Mr. Hamilton had been assigned two new students that semester. Mimi, and an Italian fellow by the name of Nicolo Maggio.

"First things first. Let's go into my lab and lets each of you play. I need to asses where you are. Nicolo went first. Mimi was impressed. She watched the dark haired young man that looked about twenty, as he sat and played for about ten minutes. She was impressed. His style was a bit different than hers. And she noticed that when he played, he slumped over his keyboard. Something she knew would horrify Miss. Bierman! Then it was her turn. She took her seat and began to play Moonlight Serenade. The professor listened intently as did Nicolo, who sat there with an astonished look on his face.

"Miss Bennis, just how old are you?" Questioned Mr. Hamilton.

"Sixteen Sir. I'm sixteen."

"Well I must say, I didn't expect to hear that coming from you. You are definitely some kind of prodigy. Wouldn't you agree Mr. Maggio? How long have you been playing?"

"Ever since I can remember Sir. I started to play sitting on my mother's lap have been playing ever since. I've been working very hard at my lessons. My family has always made sure that I had great teachers. My last teacher was Ariana Bierman. Do you know her?"

"I most certainly do! She's a very good friend of mine. We go back a long time. I'm surprised she didn't mention you to me but perhaps she didn't want to influence me in any way. I'll make sure that I let her know that you are one of my new students. Well, this is what we're going to do. I will work with you Mr. Maggio in the mornings from eight until eleven AM. We'll break two hours for lunch, and then Miss Bennis I will work with you until four. I expect you both to be on time all the time. There is no excuse for tardiness or absence. Unless there is blood or death, I expect you to be at your keyboard every day. Do you have any questions? My telephone number is on the chalkboard. Write it down. Do not use it unless it is absolutely necessary. Save your questions until you meet with me. You're both excused. You're welcome to stay and practice in one of the rehearsal rooms for the rest of the day. There is a file folder on the piano each of your names on them. That is what you will be working on first. I cannot express the importance of practice, practice, practice. If at any time I feel that you are not keeping up with your studies I will see to it that you are dismissed from the Conservatory. There are a great many students waiting to come here. If you're not willing to put in the work we will certainly make room for them. Don't make me have to send you home. Good day."

"Wow what was that?" Said Nicolo as he turned to look at Mimi. "My name is Nicolo Maggio it's a pleasure to make your acquaintance." He said with an Italian accent. I noticed that you have a slight accent. Where you from." He questioned.

"I'm from Cuba. I came on one of the Peter Pan flights last year. I'm living here in New York with my foster family, Mr. and Mrs. Boxwell. Where are you from?"

"My family is from *Roma.* Rome as they say in America. I come from a long line of pianists and pizza makers. I'm staying with my uncle Marco. My parents sent me to live with him while I go to school here at Julliard. But I also have to work in the pizzeria. My uncle Marco says 'there's no such thing as a free ride in America'. So when I'm not studying and flipping the dough, I'm washing the pots in the kitchen. It's much cooler in here than at the restaurant. It's nice that they have the air conditioning- eh?"

Mimi laughed. "I don't think I've ever had pizza, is it good?"

"Is it good? It's the best! You must bring your family to Marcos. It's just four blocks east of here. Come on Sundays. That's when I'm working there. The rest of the time I'm upstairs on the keyboard."

"I'll mention it to them of course. Maybe we can come soon. I think I'm going to step into the practice room and use that piano so that you can use this one. I'd like to go ahead and look at the music sheets before I go home and see what he's throwing at us. It's very nice meeting you. It will be nice studying with you too. Goodbye."

"Ciao Bella."

Mimi walked into the room adjacent to the one they were in and closed the door behind her. She hadn't been exposed to soundproof rooms before and was amazed that she couldn't hear Nicolo playing beyond the glass. She took a seat on the bench in front of the grand piano and sat with her back towards Nicolo. She looked around the small room and noticed that it was covered in white acoustic panels, and between both rooms there was a very thick plate of glass dividing them. She opened up the folder that Professor Hamilton had given each one each of them. Studying the notes on the paper she realized she was not familiar with this music. She began to play and practice the worksheet she'd been given. Before she knew it, it was 4 o'clock. She thought she'd better hurry if she was going to catch the train back home. She couldn't wait to get there and tell the Boxwells all about her day. It was very exciting to finally be at the school she'd heard so much about and was so grateful for the opportunity to study there. She felt so mature riding the train home alone. And she couldn't wait to write her friend Dolores

and tell her all about it. Mimi was having to grow up in a
hurry.

Chapter 20

Mimi progressed very rapidly in her classes. Professor Hamilton was so impressed that he asked her to join one of the Chamber Music groups much earlier than usual. She worked long hours and practice constantly. Her first performance was to be of all places, Carnegie Hall during the Christmas Season. She was to play along with four other students during a special performance of The Nutcracker. The thought of playing on that stage was very meaningful to her. She remembered when she was younger, the stories her Abuela would tell her of attending performances there whenever she and her Abuelo would come for visits to New York. She'd seen pictures of the inside and of the grand and famous stage. She'd always wanted to play there.

These days she was practically living at Julliard. On top of her demanding piano schedule, she had to take other classes that were required for her degree several days of the week for two hours. So she would make up the time by getting there early and leaving late. Professor Hamilton was very demanding and he'd accept nothing but perfection from his new students.

Nicolo was also immensely intelligent and quite talented. It was good for Mimi because the friendly completion kept her on her toes. They had become good friends. On the days they could steal away for a few minutes, they would walk together to Central Park during their lunch breaks and quiz one another for their class exams. They were taking Music History and Music Theory. Two of the many classes they would have to pass to get that degree. It was the only time the two of them would see the sunlight. Their hours were very draining. Especially for Nicolo who was expected to clean the kitchen at the restaurant every day when he got home regardless of what time.

Finally, the day came to go for rehearsals to Carnegie. Mimi was beyond excited. Her first big performance in front of an audience other than the friends of families of the students. When she arrived at fifty seventh and seventh, she knew she was early. She'd given herself a few extra minutes so she could find the back entrance to the stage. There was a guard with a list of the people that had permission to enter. Once she checked in, she followed a couple of other musicians through the sea of winding props and curtains and on to the stage. Once she arrived, it was mouth dropping! The luxurious red velvet seats went as far back as she could see. There were not one, but four balconies!   She almost had to pinch herself. It looked exactly like the pictures in the photo albums back home. It was huge! She stood there taking it all in before she heard someone call her name. One of the musicians she'd be playing with was in the orchestra pit waving her down.   She made her way to them. They told her they were waiting for Professor Hamilton. He would be conducting them for the rehearsal. Mimi walked over to the Grand Steinway Piano and took a seat on the bench. The other musicians had all arrived early as well and had begun to warm up, so she joined them.

She could barely keep her eyes on the music sheets. She was still looking around and so wished that her Abuela could see her. And she knew her Mami would be very proud of her. Finally, Mr. Hamilton arrived and began the rehearsal. They ran for four hours before he dismissed them. He told them he'd expect them tomorrow at the same time. He felt they were a bit *off* because they weren't used to the acoustics of the auditorium. So was going to work with them another day. The first performance was that same weekend and he wanted and expected perfection.   Mimi was the youngest of the musicians there.   She knew he expected her to stay focused and be at her best.

When Saturday afternoon came, Mimi began to finally

feel the pressure. She and Mrs. Boxwell had gone to purchase a long black skirt and a white silk blouse to wear. She got dressed and began to fuss with her hair, but her fingers were all thumbs. Mrs. Boxwell saw this and said.

"Let me pull your hair back with a ribbon so it doesn't get into your face while you are playing. It'll make you more comfortable and it's one less thing to worry about on stage."

When she finished, she offered Mimi some lipstick to wear and they used some compact powder on her face.

"You look so grown up! Our Princess is growing up."

When Mrs. Boxwell said this to her, it brought back memories of how the kids at the camp would tease her when she first arrived. *Boy if those mean girls could see me now!* She thought.

Mr. and Mrs. Boxwell were attending the first performance that evening. They were going to ride in with her so they could all go get an early dinner. Mimi didn't touch her food. Her stomach was in knots. She left them at the restaurant to make her way to the hall early. They still had plenty of time, so they stayed for desert.

Once they were in their seats, they were just as excited as Mimi was. They were seated in the first balcony, second row. Great seats to see the performance, and the acoustics were better there than on the main level.

Mimi walked into the orchestra pit with the other musicians from Julliard who were playing along with her. Her nerves had finally calmed down now that she was seated at the piano. She felt a bit more in control once she could touch the keys. Everyone went through the warm up routine and before she knew it, the conductor was on at his podium. The place went silent, and he gave his first command. The curtain opened and the performance was on its way. Mimi was too focused to worry about anything that was going on up on the stage. And when it was over, she got to stand and take her first professional bow. She was hooked! The adrenalin that overtook her at that moment was like a bolt of lightning. *This* is where she belonged. Performing in front of a real live audience. She was never more grateful for all of the piano classes she had endured as a little girl. It had all paid off.

That evening when they all got home, Mimi was too wound up to sleep. Mrs. Boxwell brought her a cup of hot cocoa. It hadn't started to snow yet, but you could feel it in the air. They all sat in the living room near the fire and talked until well into the night before they all got sleepy. There were two performances tomorrow, and four the following weekend. Mimi couldn't wait to get back on that stage. She told the Boxwells about the photo album back home. They listened as she went on about her life in Cuba. It was the first time she had actually opened up to them about growing up, and how after her mami's death she'd been sent to live at the plantation with her grandparents. She told them about the tobacco and described the beautiful valley she grew up in. She described the Royal Palms and how they rustled outside of her bedroom window at night when the wind caught their leaves. She even shared with them about the boy who held a special place in her heart. They realized that she needed to get these things off her chest. And that by doing so, she was letting them in. They knew she trusted them, and that they now felt like family to her.

Mr. Boxwell asked her what she saw in her future. And *that* of course, was to become a great pianist. They had no doubt she would accomplish it, and were so happy that they were going to be part of her dream.

Mimi kept to her commitment of hard work and study, and her time at Julliard flew by. Before she knew it, it was the end of her last semester. She'd performed with several of the Philharmonics and had traveled to many states and countries to perform with many major orchestras. Now twenty years old, in the music world she was considered a Virtuoso. Graduation was staring her in the face and the tickets that featured her as a guest pianist were becoming harder and harder to come by.

Mimi had made many friends along the way and had been tempted by many of the male students. But somehow, she didn't feel like any of them were right for her. She had grown into a beautiful young woman with a body to die for. He long brown hair sat at her waist. Her skin was flawless, and her smile was constant. Her big beautiful brown eyes glistened when she smiled. Everyone loved her. She was kind and considerate. Always lending a hand when anyone needed help.

Her friendship with Nicolo had remained strong. They had formed a special bond, and although he was quite the ladies' man, they maintained their friendship and respect for one another. He had become like a brother to her and they trusted each other with their feelings and secrets. Aside from Dolores, he was her 'go to person' if she ever needed any advice. They kept nothing from one another.

Mimi had confided in him that she had been approached by the New York Philharmonic to join them on a tour that fall following graduation. But she'd been tempted to go London to perform with the symphony there. She thought it would be exciting to live in a different country for a while and travel while she was still young. Nicolo had already accepted a job with the Vienna

Philharmonic and was looking forward to never having to wash another pizza tray as long as he lived! A real feather in his cap considering how difficult it was to obtain a chair with them. But they had approached him, and he jumped at the chance. This would at least get him on the other side of the pond and closer to his family in Rome. Mimi expressed her concern of leaving the Boxwells after all they had done for her, but he reassured her that he knew for a fact that her happiness was always first on their minds and in their hearts. And that they would always be her family.

So, in October of 1967, Mimi left the family and the place she considered home, and set off on the next adventure. Unsure what was waiting for her. But knowing that if she could start again at age fifteen, she could certainly do it again at twenty. She began her future in London where she made a good life for herself. She traveled all over the world and performed for dignitaries, queens and kings.

She played all of the world with rewound orchestras and made many recordings. Her name was known to all as the must see pianist. But after twenty years, it was time to go home again. It was time to take care of the two people who meant the most to her. She purchased an apartment in Manhattan and decided to take a break for a several years only giving select performances so she could devote time and travel with Lisa and Tom.

Chapter 21

June 1998

Life had been good to Maribel Bennis. She had spent the last several years picking and choosing her performances. Still in great demand, the Miami Symphony Orchestra had convinced her to come and perform on their stage for a charity event, in advance of the most anticipated performance by the upcoming tour of the "Buena Vista Social Club." She was going to take the stage and open the show for them at Carnegie Hall in New York on July first. The promotors of the show had sought her out due to her fame and accomplishments as one of the now grown children of the Peter Pan flights.

The Miami Symphony was holding a special concert featuring several local Latin American musicians and wanted her to participate. Being that it was for charity and the money was to go to the Miami Catholic Charities, she agreed to play and thought it would be fun to just relax and play without the pressure of the normal concert performances. She agreed to play for two nights.

As part of the promotion for the event, she'd been asked to be interviewed by one of the local television news channels. As she waited in her suite for the TV camera to set up, and the newscaster to arrive, the costume department was making the final touches on the gown she was to wear that evening. It was based on a traditional conga style dress, and it was red white and blue satin.

When the doorbell rang, the Room Valet escorted the gentleman interviewer to the living room and told him she was almost finished and would be right with out. Ricky Reyes was a very influential man who didn't like to be kept waiting. He was a Cuban born newscaster that had been with the station for over twenty years, and was well known in the Miami Dade, Ft. Lauderdale area.

Ricky walked to the balcony window, and was taking in the ocean view. He kept looking at his watch. He had a luncheon arranged later with one of the producers, and wanted to arrive on time. While he stared out, he heard a voice from behind him say.

"I'm so sorry to keep you waiting. It's hard getting out of clothes without getting stuck with pins."

Ricky turned ready to introduce himself to Miss. Bennis and stopped dead in his tracks. They both looked like they had seen a ghost. The camera man and the sound man looked back and forth between them with a puzzled look on their faces. Finally, he broke the silence.

"Mimi?" He said as his face color drained.

"Antonio? Is that you? Can it be possible?"

"*You* are the legendary Maribel Bennis? How could I

not have known this?"

Realizing something had just happened that might be newsworthy, the sound man signaled to the camera man to roll the film.

Mimi and Antonio walked towards each other and embraced. They held one another for a long time. Both had tears in their eyes.

"They told me someone from the television was coming to interview me by the name of Ricky Reyes. I knew you as Antonio."

"My full name is Antonio Enrique Reyes. When I took a professional name, it was suggested that I shorten my middle name to Ricky and use that. It seemed more mainstream America. And I only ever knew you as Mimi. I never knew your last name. It was different than your grandparents."

"My given name is Maribel Bennis. My family called me Mimi for short. How long have you been here? Please sit here by me. We must catch up."

Mimi led Antonio to the sofa and they both sat facing each other. They held hands as they talked and looked into each other's eyes. The camera crew was running the tape but they were completely unaware.

"Two of my older brothers and I came on a raft in 1966. Things became so bad we just couldn't stay any longer. We drifted for days praying the sharks wouldn't eat us. But we had decided that if that was to be our fate, it would be better to die than to give into the Regime. Our third day adrift, some American fishermen found us and dropped us off at a pier in Miami. We were able to stay because of the "wet foot, dry foot law." We found some cousins in Little Havana that came about the same time that you disappeared, and we stayed with them doing odd jobs and trying to survive. I put myself to school and became a journalist. I wanted to write about the *atrocities* that were happening to the people of our country. Becoming a journalist was the best way I could find to get my voice heard. I began as a writer for a newspaper and moved my way up. I never knew what happened to you. No one on the plantation knew. And then your grandparents died....well you know."

"They died? When did they die? How?"

Antonio realized she was unaware of their fate. He thought it best not to go into the grim details at that moment knowing that she had a performance that night, and didn't want to upset her.

"How did you get here? When did you come?" He tried to distract her and change the conversation.

"My Tia and Tio in Havana put me on one of the Peter Pan flights. They sent me to America to my father. But he wouldn't take me home. He had a new family and there was no place for me. It's a long story. We should spend some time together and talk about everything. I want to know everything. I've never forgotten you. I've thought about you over the years and wondered if you remembered me?"

"How could I not remember you? You were my first love!"

Mimi blushed. Antonio suggested they do a quick interview for the evening news and they set a date to have lunch the next day not aware of all the camera had caught. After the interview, Mimi had to get ready for the show so Antonio left. He was emotionally charged from what had just happened. She was walking on a cloud! A feeling of happiness had filled her heart like she'd never felt before. At last, she had found her one true love. So many things were going through her mind at that moment. She wondered if there could be a future for them. But she knew this was silly thinking. They had been children when the two of them had last been together. This was another time and certainly another place. But it gave her such a great feeling inside. Like she'd been given *something* back from her young adult life. Something that had been taken away so abruptly. The promise of hope is what made her so happy.

Once they arrived at the TV station, Antonio reviewed the film and threatened the two guys that had been on the crew. He was upset they had filmed his meeting with Mimi, and told them that this had been a private moment. He would never publicize any of it. But he kept the film anyway. Afterwards he decided to pull some strings. He called one of the station assistants and got a ticket to Mimi's performance that evening. He didn't want her to know he was there, but knew he had to see her play. His memory of her playing at the Plantation on Sunday afternoons came back to him, and he wanted to re live those moments.

The show went off without a hitch. Mimi played to a packed audience and at the end, everyone got a standing ovation. This performance was different than the ones that Mimi usually played. Being a classically trained pianist, her repertoire was always filled with Bach, Beethoven and Tchaikovsky. But tonight was a lighter flair. She would join the symphony for a throwback to old Broadway show hits. So she was just going to enjoy herself. She was also looking forward to her trip back to New York to open for the Buena Vista Social Club.

These were men and women that had been rediscovered in Havana by a couple of American music producer on a trip to Cuba. They found these musicians, most of them now in their seventies and eighties, that had been well known in the Golden Era of music in the nineteen forties and fifty's. They convinced them to come out of retirement and record again. Many of them were reluctant at first. They didn't think they would be able to perform. But once they got together and began playing, it was as if no time had passed. The album became an international best seller and even won a Grammy. They had become so sought after, that the Cuban government gave special permission and allowed them travel to America to perform. And on July first, Mimi was to join them on stage for the opening of the show. She was excited to meet them and felt it would be an honor to share the stage with them. She didn't know yet what she would play. But she knew it would come to her.

Chapter 22

The next morning, Mimi was walking back to her suite after a quick rehearsal before the second and last show. She was then leaving for New York. She was meeting Antonio at a nearby Cuban restaurant for lunch so they could catch up. She could hardly breathe with excitement. As her limo pulled up, he stood waiting outside for her. He greeted her with a hug and a kiss on the cheek. Totally a Cuban thing to do! Kisses on the cheek are a sign of affection.

Mimi knew she probably wasn't going to be able to eat much, but Cuban food was hard to come by in New York. So she was going to try. He had requested a booth near the back of the restaurant so they would have less chance of being recognized and could have some privacy. After glancing at the menu and placing an order, Ricky poured some wine he had ordered and he toasted to their chance meeting.

Antonio couldn't keep his eyes off of her. She looked exactly the same. Same beautiful eyes, same beautiful long hair. And her smile was brighter than ever.

Mimi thought he looked even more handsome than

ever. He had outgrown that awkward thin form most guys have at that age. He had filled out and turned into a very handsome man. Still had a full head of hair with just a slight dusting of silver at the temples.

Mimi began telling him about the events that led her to America. And of her Grandparents rush to get her out of the country and onto the Peter Pan flight. Then, she explained the difficulties she encountered at her first foster home, to the blessing of the Boxwells, who she now considered to be her parents. She told him about her studies at Julliard and the move to London where she lived and traveled for twenty years. She was also honest with him about the relationships she had had with several musicians and others in the music world. But was never really able to solidify into a lifelong commitment for whatever reason. She told him that she always wondered if Castro hadn't come to turn their country upside down, *'what if'* would have happened between them.

Then it was his turn to talk. The first thing he talked to her about was of the death of her grandparents. But he had decided to leave out the part of the disposition of their remains after they met their deaths in the hands of that revolutionary. He'd given it some thought after their meeting the day before, and had decided nothing good would come out of her knowing. So he spared her those details.

"The revolutionary who took over the Tobacco Plantation ended up dragging it to ruins. He was a heartless man who was cruel to the workers and his family. He beat them, starved them and some were executed as examples of what would happen if they didn't do as they were told. My brothers and I couldn't take it anymore. So we took our chances. We made a raft at night and hid it during the day until we could finish it. One of my uncles was a fisherman and knew the tides. He told us when it was better to leave. And we got on our way during the new moon when it was dark so we would have less of a chance to be seen. All we had with us was some coconuts and a jug with water. Finally on the third day, we got lucky and got to shore. "

He confessed to having been married once, but it only lasted three years. He has a son in Tampa who is married. And he confessed that his new notoriety had given him the opportunity to meet and be with many women. But that at this stage of his life, he was looking for someone to share forever with. And he was ready.

"You coming back into my life right now is not a coincidence. I believe that everything happens for a reason don't you? "

Their meeting had gone on for several hours. Mimi

realized she needed to go or she would be late for the show. She still had to pack so she could leave for the airport right from the performance that night. She was taking the red eye. Mimi invited Antonio to see her in concert with The Buena Vista group and told him she'd leave a ticket at 'will call' for him so he could be sure and get in. The show had been sold out for months, but she had been given several guess passes. He assured her he wouldn't miss it.

Her limo pulled up outside of her hotel and she exited in a hurry. As she walked through the lobby, she was approached by two young Jewish men in their early forties. They both wore yamakas and payots. As they approached, one of them addressed her.

"Miss. Bennis? Are you Miss. Maribel Bennis?"

She stopped for a moment. Knowing of her Jewish heritage, she was curious as to what business these two men might have with her.

"Miss Bennis, may we have a word with you please? I think we may be your brothers."

The words hit Mimi like a freight train. She was completely taken off guard. She didn't know what to say or what to do.

"We don't want to take up too much of your time, but we have some things we think you might be interested in having. Could we go somewhere and talk?"

Mimi led them to a sofa and a group of chairs away from the main lobby area. She sat across from the two men and asked….

"Gentlemen, what's this all about?"

"Miss. Bennis. We're Adam and David Bennis. Our father, Robert Bennis recently passed away. He suffered from Parkinson's disease. On his death bed, he talked to us about *you*. You see, our mother was a very strict woman who had an iron hand in their marriage. We'd heard rumors that we had a Cuban sister from some members of the family, but knowing how she was, no one would ever elaborate on this. When our father was near the end, he told us the story of how he met your mother, and of his great love for her. He shared with us about her tragic death. Papa explained of how he fled to America with our grandparents during the communist takeover, and that you had been left in the care of your grandparents. Papa told us where to find this shoe box and asked that we find you and give it to you. We gave him our word. "

One of the young men handed Mimi an old shoe box. She lifted the lid and saw it was filled with all kinds of newspaper articles about her. There were also torn theater tickets, and some old *Air Mail* envelopes containing letters.

"Papa told us to tell you that the letters were found in our mothers personal things when she passed. Apparently these letters had come addressed to him from your relatives, and she hid them. He never knew about them until he stumbled on after her death them while cleaning out her dresser. There is one more thing: there is a velvet box inside. He wanted to make sure you were given that box."

The younger of the two men reached in and brought out a beautiful velvet box, then handed it to Mimi. She stared at it for a moment and then opened it. Inside, she saw that it contained her mother's diamond brooche. She remembered her mother wearing it all the time and often wondered what had happened to it. She thought it must have gotten lost after she left home.

"Papa wanted us to tell you he had never forgotten you. And that he loved you very much. But so much time had passed, that when our mother died he didn't have the heart to disrupt your life. He thought you hated him and he didn't want to die with the memory of you telling him that. He asked that you forgive him.

We hope you'll think about calling us some time if you feel that you'd like to get to know the other half of your family. We'd love to have you become part of our lives. Here is a card with a number you can all next time you're in Florida. It was good meeting you in person." The card read – "Bennis Fine Diamonds" with an address and phone number.

Both of the men stood and shook hands with Mimi. She was still seated and unable to move when they left.

What just happened? She thought to herself. Glancing at her watch, she realized she would have to deal with this latter if she was going to make curtain call. She rushed upstairs and put the box inside of her makeup case, finished packing and quickly put on her costume. She wouldn't have time to change into it at the theater.

Chapter 23

It was about one thirty in the morning when the jet bound for New York left Ft. Lauderdale airport. Mimi was exhausted. These had been two of the most emotionally charged days of her adult life. Her meeting with her childhood sweetheart had brought her heart joy. And now, the meeting with the two men claiming to be the two brothers she didn't even know she had…she didn't know what to think.

After the plane had reached cruising altitude, Mimi unbuckled her seatbelt and reached into the overhead compartment to retrieve her makeup case. She opened it and took out the shoe box she had crammed inside. Placing the box on her lap, she began to look through the contents. Inside, she found old newspaper clippings that featured articles of the many awards she had received over the years. Articles of her performances for the Queen of England. And when she played at the White House for the President, as well as many dignitaries from all over the world. She even found tickets to some of her performances in Florida, New York and Chicago. She assumed he must have secretly attended and never told anyone. It was like a time capsule of her life. He must have had these hidden away from his wife. The wife that didn't want him to have anything to do with her.

Then, there were the letters. They had obviously been opened and read because the top had been torn. They were all from her Tia in Havana. Reading her name on the return address portion of the envelope brought tears to Mimi's eyes. She pressed the letters against her chest and began to cry. At last. She knew they hadn't forgotten her. She finally had validation.

Her hands began to shake as she pulled out the lightweight onion skin paper that had been used in those days for Airmail letters to save on mailing costs. The letter was brief and to the point.

"Dearest Robert, We pray this letter finds you and your parents safe and well. I'm writing to you to make sure you are aware that this morning, we put Mimi on one of the Pan American planes with the 'Peter Pan' children to Miami. Not having your telephone number in America, this is the only way we have of contacting you. The communist are no longer allow us to send telegrams. She left today, July 14. As you know, it's also her fifteenth birthday. She was sent there with the help of the Catholic Diocese, who is taking care of the children until their families can come to get them. If they haven't contacted you, please go find her! Thank you Robert. We love you and miss hearing from you. Be well. Love, Tia Rosa - P.S. Make sure she practices the piano."

Mimi smiled when she read the P.S. part of the letter. It was very much her Tia's sense of humor.

She carefully folded the fragile piece of paper and put it back into the envelope. Then she read the second letter. This one was dated about two months after the first one.

"Dearest Robert, We haven't had any word from you and we're worried sick about Mimi. I say a Rosary every day for her and pray that she is at your side. We wanted to let you know that Mimi's grandparents are dead. They were shot and killed at the plantation by a man from the militia who has confiscated the land. We hope you can find the words to tell her. Thing have really gotten bad here very fast. Food is being rationed. There is no power much of the time. Tio Javier is being forced to work for the government now, and as much as we would like to leave to join you and Mimi, I'm afraid it's not to be. The government is not going to allow any more Doctors to leave the country. Everything and everyone is being controlled. You can't even talk to your neighbors anymore because you don't know if they are *for or against* the revolution, and will turn you in, in exchange for extra food rations. Please take care of Mimi and tell her how very much we love her. Be well. Love, Tia Rosa."

Reading the words describing her beloved grandparents' death made Mimi sick. She felt like she wanted to die right there. She cradled the letter close to her heart and sobbed. The flight attendant came by and asked her if she was ok. She asked for a Brandy and told her she would be alright.

Then, the third letter. She was almost afraid to open it. She dreaded knowing what fate had brought to them. She waited for the Brandy to come and took a drink to try and steady her shaky hands. She took a deep breath and unfolded the paper. It read:

"Dearest Robert, I'm not sure if this letter will get to you or not. The communists are censoring all of the correspondence to and from here. They're especially monitoring us because Javier is a Doctor, and want to make sure he isn't plotting against them in any way or planning to escape the island. One of the Doctors who's been a friend of ours all our lives, and his family attempted to leave on a boat but were found out. The entire family was executed. Since we haven't heard from you or Mimi we're not sure if my letters are getting to you. But I will continue to write as long as I can. And I will continue to pray for all of you too. Also, the bad news I have for you this time is devastating. Javier was diagnosed with cancer and isn't expected to live very long. I don't know what is to become of me when he dies. Please give Mimi our love and know you are all in our hearts and in our prayers. Be well. Love, Tia Rosa- P.S. Please tell Mimi to be sure and practice her piano lessons."

This one really devastated Mimi. She downed the rest of the Brandy and asked for a second one. She finally had some news of her family, and now wondered if it wouldn't have been better not knowing at all.

Mimi put the letters back in the box and put it away. She turned her face towards the window. There was nothing to see in the darkness but an occasional tiny blinking light down below. Most of the flight was over the ocean. But she really wasn't looking to see anything. She just wanted to continue to cry and not have anyone see her breaking down. She couldn't wait to get home. All she wanted to do now was scream at the top of her lungs.

The next day, Mimi went to visit the Boxwells. They sat at the dining room table and she shared what had happened with them. They cried with her and held her hands. She had been so very lucky to have found them and have them in her life. But they felt *she* had been the blessing in theirs. With her, they had become a real family. She'd always been very good to them too.

~ ~ ~ ~ ~ ~ ~ ~ ~

The night of the performance was finally here. The whole city was abuzz about the Buena Vista Social Club. People had seen them all over town shopping and signing autographs. They had been interviewed by newspapers and magazines. Mimi was delighted to be opening the show for them. She felt that being asked to play on their stage was a great honor. She'd come full circle now. She finally had closure on the life she left behind, *and* was looking forward to what lay ahead with her new re-found love. The bellman called her apartment to let her know the limo had arrived. She grabbed her garment bag with the new dress and makeup bag. She was really looking forward to the evening.

When she arrived at the stage entrance to the theater, she was mobbed by fans asking for her autograph. Flashes from cameras were blinding her as she made her way in through the back door of the theater. She went inside and straight in to meet all of the performers. They told her how proud they were of her and of what she'd done with her life. But Mimi hugged them all and told them that *they* were her inspiration and that it was a great pleasure to be there that evening and play with them. Fame hadn't changed the kind, shy, humble little girl. She was just doing what she loved to do.

Inside her dressing room, there were flowers everywhere. But on her makeup table, there was a round glass bowl filled with Gardenias and a note. "We have the rest of our lives. Amor, Antonio." Of all the arrangements, this was the one she loved the most.

Mimi heard a knock at the door and shouted to 'come in.' It was Dolores. The girls hadn't seen each other since Christmas when they had dinner during a visit to New York.

"You look beautiful!" She said to her friend. "You look like you're glowing! What's going on? Here sit, let me do our hair. Tonight you have your own personal beautician. Tell me all about it"

Dolores had indeed become a beautician. Mimi had helped her pay for school and she was now married with two kids. A son and a daughter. Everyone was there to see the performance. As she sat there getting her hair done, Mimi told her best friend all about the recent events and how life changing they had all been. She was in shock when she told her about her family in Cuba, but was very happy to hear she had found her first love and that the two of them were going to re kindle their romance. Then she left to take her seat along with her family.

Mimi put on a new black velvet dress. She retouched

her make up, and as she looked in the mirror, put on the finishing touch. Her mother's diamond brooch. She stood back and looked at its reflection in the mirror. She said a little prayer and asked her Mami to look after her on stage that evening.

When the moment arrived, Mimi was called on stage and as she was introduced. She walked onto the stage to a full house. Carnegie Hall. The grand theater she had always treasured had seemed even more special that night. All 2,804 seats were full. The sound of the applause was deafening. Seated in the front row, she could see Dolores and her family along with her parents. The Boxwells with Mrs. Shear sat right alongside of them.

Mimi took her seat on the piano bench and adjusted it. It was amazing how quickly silence came over the crowd. You could hear a pin drop. She had selected the song she was going to play weeks before. But at that moment, it didn't seem quite right. With her eyes now closed and taking deep breaths, she felt as if her hands being taken over. It was just like when she was a little girl again, and she was seated on her mother's lap. Her hands on hers.

When she began to play, the applause rang out again for a minute. The song she was playing was, 'Sabor a Mi'. It was that very romantic song her mother used to play for her father when she was little. She raised her head as she played. She saw Antonio standing in the wing of the theater watching her. He was wearing a black tuxedo and a huge smile. But that wasn't the only thing she could see. As she played, there at the end of the beautiful grand piano, stood her smiling parents, her grandparents and her aunt and uncle. Their presence was with her on the stage along with her at that moment. Her heart was full.

Halfway through the song, the sound of a crisp loud trumpet joined her on the stage along with a guitarist. Both of the older gentlemen apparently touched by her music had come out early to help her finish the song. And before she knew it, the entire Buena Vista Social Club had taken the stage with Mimi. Including a singer, who was now singing the lyrics. Everyone was transcended through time to another place, another era. And for those few minutes, time stood still, and magic filled everyone in that concert hall. The crowd went crazy, and they played two more bars of the song.

By the time she had finished, everyone was on the stage along with her. But this wasn't *her* night. This night belonged to the other musicians there with her, whose lives had been disrupted like hers. Just like the millions of others or who had been left behind. And the many that were forced to leave, and whose lives were forced to take a different course.

Mimi stood and took a bow to a roaring crowd. The entire concert hall was on their feet. And as she prepared to walk off, she waved at the audience, and then made a waving motion to the musicians as if to say, *the stage is yours*.

As she walked off, Mimi knew she was leaving her past on that stage that night. And she knew she was walking towards her future, who was waiting with opened arms for her in the wings.

Fin

Sabor a Mi

Written by: Alvaro Carrillo Alarcon

Tanto tiempo disfrutamos de este Amor

--For so long we have enjoyed this love

Nuestras almas se acercaron tanto asi

--Our souls got so close

Que you guardo tu sabor

--That I keep you taste

Pero tu llevas tambien

--but you also carry

Sabor a mi

--A taste of me.

Si negaras mi presencia en tu vivir

-If you would deny my presence in your life

Bastaria con abrazarte y conversar

--It would suffice to embrace you and talk

Tanta vida yo te di

--so much of my life I gave to you

Que por fuerza tienes ya

--That you can't help but have

Sabor a mi

--A taste of me

No pretend ser tu dueño

--I am not trying to be your owner

No soy nada, yo no tengo vanidad

--I am nothing, I have no vanity

De mi vida, doy lo Bueno

--Of my life, I give the good

Soy tan pobre que otra cosa puedo dar?

--I am so poor, what else can I give?

Pasaran mas te mill años, muchos mas

--A thousand years may pass, many more

Yo no se si tenga Amor la eternidad

--I don't know if love exists in eternity

Pero alla tal como aqui

--But there just as here

En la boca llevaras

--In your mouth you will carry

Sabor a mi

--A taste of me

Arroz con Pollo

My Mother Zoila's recipe

About two chickens cut into pieces
1 – 8 oz. can or bottle of beer
½ Cup of olive oil
1 large bay leaves
4-5 garlic cloves – smashed
2 cups chicken broth
1 bitter orange
1 teaspoon of salt
1 large onion chopped
1 large bell pepper chopped
1 small can of peas
2 Tablespoons of tomato paste
1 regular size can of tomato sauce
1 small jar of pimento-cooked red bell pepper
2 cups of cooked rice
¼ teaspoon of Bijol (or Saffron if available)
1 jar of Spanish olives

In a large oven proof pan, combine onion, garlic, tomato paste, tomato sauce, and bell pepper. Cook on low until soft. Add chicken and cook on both sides for about four minutes per side. Add cooked rice and the remaining ingredients, minus the pimento. Bring to a boil and cover. Bake in oven at 350 degrees for forty five minutes to an hour depending on your oven's cooking time. Remove the lid, decorate the top with slices of the pimento and serve right away. Enjoy!

Made in the USA
Columbia, SC
25 September 2017